DEDICATION

To my late father Iorwa Akpeghe

ACKNOWLEDGEMENT

I want to specially acknowledge my elder brother, Fr Michael Iorwa who created the right atmosphere for me to make this project a reality.

I acknowledge family and friends who in one way or the other were instrumental in the realization of this work.

TABLE OF CONTENTS

Chapter One

We sat beside each other as we watched a home video. My heart pounded rapidly as I sat close to him. I could tell deep down within me that I had fallen in love yet again. He simply sat beside me like a log of wood, focusing all his attention to the movie.

"What is wrong with this boy?" I wondered unhappily.

"Doesn't he seem attracted to me the way I feel for him?" I began asking myself questions I couldn't give answers to.

That day was the third time I was spending my afternoon with him yet, he failed to notice my passes and acted like he had never developed any feelings for any lady before.

Samuel was an attractive wealthy male who caught my fancy right from the first day I packed into the new lodge. Unlike most guys, he kept to himself and behaved like a saint, winning my heart with his godly behavior. But getting him to reciprocate my good gestures towards him was a very hard task.

His intense behavior soon began irritating me, forcing me to make up my mind not to visit him again after that Tuesday evening. I had my pride to protect which, really, was more important than my interest in him.

He was in his 300 level, while I was in my second year in the University. My feelings for him were really strong and divine, but I couldn't display my emotions the way I wanted, without appearing cheap and disgusting.

Finally by 8pm, the movie ended. I sighed and got up from his chair.

"Good night," I said to him unhappily, but surprisingly, he held my hand strongly and looked up at me with fire in his eyes.

"Please don't go yet, there is something I wish to tell you," he pleaded. I gazed into his eyes and smiled,

"Finally he is living up to expectation," I reasoned.

"Please sit down," he begged humbly. I rolled my eyes and sat beside him

"I know you do trust me a lot, that's why I'm the only guy you always visit, but I can't help it anymore. I have tried to suppress my feelings but I can't any longer, because it's killing me silently. I have been dreaming and praying to have someone like you. Please will you grant my request and be my special friend?" "I have been in love with you from the very first day I saw you," he pleaded nervously with shaking lips. I stared at him coldly even though I was very happy within.

"I don't think it will be possible. Let's just be friends," I replied and stood up. He tried to draw my hand, but I snatched it from his grasp.

"Goodnight we will see tomorrow," I murmured, gave him one last look and left for my room.

I rushed to my room, hugged my teddy bear happily, and heaved a sigh of relief.

I was very delighted.

"At last, hmmm," I murmured and sighed happily, falling asleep and dreaming of good times.

By 6am the following morning, I heard a gentle knock on my door and when I got to the door, there stood Samuel, hands in his trouser pocket, smiling at me.

"Good morning," I greeted and yawned.

"I'm so sorry for disturbing you this early, it's just that I was unable to sleep all through last night," he explained nervously.

I let him into my room. He settled on my chair and kept me company, while I brushed and freshened up.

"Seriously, I still find it hard to chat with you," he confessed, making me giggle and laugh.

"But I don't think it is a good thing to be shy before a girl, moreover we do like guys who are manly," I advised jokingly. He smiled and stared at me.

"Hope I didn't put you off with my behavior yesterday?" he asked curiously,

"I'm so sorry about it," he apologized with a drawn face. I breathed deeply, summoned courage, advanced towards him and planted a kiss on his cheek which left him totally surprised.

"Let's forget about last night," I murmured. He stared at me with a coloured face filled up with surprise.

I really forced myself to plant the kiss on his cheek in order for him to feel free with me.

Seriously I have never met a complete introvert like Samuel before, "perhaps he might have no relationship experience before," I reasoned.

I sat on my bed that beautiful morning with a calm smile, looking up at him our eyes met.

He opened his mouth to say something, but no voice came out. He swallowed hard in embarrassment and got up.

"Are you going back to your room," I asked anxiously, he nodded in agreement.

"Yeah, I didn't warm my soup last night, let me go and check if it hasn't gone bad," he managed to mutter before leaving. I looked away unhappily, even though I didn't make it look obvious that I was unhappy.

Samuel, really, was the kind of guy most ladies do dream of having, not only because he was good looking and wealthy, he also was the quiet type. I knew he felt something for me, but the problem was just his manner of approach. He was scared of making the first move, which was then left in my hands to encourage him decently, because I had fallen for him already.

By 12 noon, I went over to my best friend's room, where I collected three local movies, while she teased me,

"Woman, you prefer watching movies alone with that your hostel boyfriend who doesn't talk to anyone ahbi?" she joked, I laughed.

"Does it concern you?" I asked and rolled my eyes. She sighed playfully.

Mariam was my very good friend, and the only girl who really knew much about my lifestyle, but however, she had one problem. She was a guy freak, which easily fell for guys and engages in ungodly activities.

Though she already had suffered a lot in their hands, she still kept on giving herself away so easily. She was living with her guy James, who equally was the person who helped me secure my hostel accommodation. Notwithstanding she was a very nice girl with a soft nature, who sacrificed her happiness for others.

With three CD Plates in my hand, I walked straight to Samuel's room. He happily let me in, devouring me with his eyes as I settled down.

I sat on the floor and watched the movies, hoping he would make advances once again. I knew, my behavior appeared desperate, but I did what I did because I had to.

I just sat and waited with a pounding heart.

I was watching the last movie when I noticed him sit beside me on the floor, with two bottles of coke and a packet of crackers biscuits, which made me smile to myself, as I focused all my attention on the movie which was showing on his television.

"Mary, here is cola oo," he managed to joke while I smiled, and looked at him in appreciation. We ate the biscuits and drank the coke in silence, as I returned my focus back to the movie once again.

He later held my hand gently, which really made me look at him with surprise, and he appealed to me with his eyes.

"Please accept me into your life, I'm not a bad person, I promise and swear to keep your dignity and respect intact. I truly love you," he begged.

"Really," I asked, while he held my hand strongly.

"I swear," he answered. I rolled my eyes and said nothing.

"Please answer me," he pleaded desperately.

Seeing him beg me really gladdened my heart, but I just pretended as if he was disturbing my peace. Yeah, that's what every girl does.

"What do you want me to say again?" I asked, while he drew his face closer to mine.

"Please just say yes," he whispered. I looked into his eyes and saw love, desire and honesty but I got hold of myself and looked away.

"Just give me time, I will think about it." I replied

But surprisingly and out of nowhere, he drew closer to me and gave me a tight hug, this I received while I closed my eyes.

But I soon got myself and gently pushed him away, while he looked at me gratefully, and with shinning eyes.

"I have never felt this way before, thank you," he said, while I looked away and closed my eyes briefly, because I equally felt something strong when we hugged, which I had never felt for any guy before, not even my last boyfriend.

I was unable to concentrate on the remaining part of the movie I was watching after the hug, because all my thoughts were now on him, and even though I was the one who pushed him away, I still wanted him to hug and hold me closer to himself, but then I had to control myself, because I was but a humble girl who had her pride and dignity to protect, and so I stood up minutes later, while he stared at me with his innocent face which always made me lose focus.

"Let me go and sleep, I'm so tired," I said to him with a smile, while he stood up as well and held my hand.

"Will you come once you wake?" he asked with a pleading face, while I looked down.

"I will try," I replied, but instead of letting me go, he drew closer to me, and hugged me again, while my soul melted. I immediately fled his room without looking back.

Chapter Two

As I lay on my bed that evening, I battled with my thoughts and emotions as I prayed for him to be real, because I really didn't want to repeat the mistake I made with my Ex-boyfriend, who had equally looked so honest when I first met him, and so in love, I was with him then, that I freely gave him my virginity.

Tears fell off my eyes as I remembered how he took my most precious possession, and I swallowed hard as I bit my lips. I knew I could never get over that trauma, because I knew the pain I passed through that fateful night. I thought he really loved me, just because he looked decent and said those words I wished to hear. I guess that's one problem every girl faces because we never really can tell or know the guy who really loves us. Moreover, they all appear good and decent at first sight, that you won't really see the wolf in them, if you also do have feelings for them which will then blind you from his faults and before you know it, he's had his way with you and it's already too late.

My thoughts really drew so many tears from my eyes that evening, and before I knew what was happening, I was already crying deeply, as my mind journeyed back to how I lost my pride to Emmanuel.

It was really something that touched my soul, spirit and body, but I didn't know it was just a game to him. Only God will judge us all and here is the story of how I lost my treasure.

I still vividly remember that fateful night as if it was yesterday. The day I thought I was doing the right thing for the guy I loved and adored.

That fateful day was February 14th of my first year in the University, and I was a simple naive virgin who knew not that a guy could go any length just to take a woman's most cherished treasure.

Emmanuel and I had dated for a year and three months prior to that particular day, and even though I felt strongly for him, I never allowed him to go beyond kissing me, and he never bothered to go further, because according to him, he valued me more than satisfying his urge, which I totally fell for, coupled with his gentle nature and behavior, without knowing that I was digging my own pit.

On that fateful Valentine's Day, he took me shopping, where he bought few clothes which he could afford for me, before treating me to a delicious meal in Chicken Republic, which was one of the best restaurants available in our vicinity that year. We really spent much time there, eating, joking and taking pictures. I must confess he really spent a lot on me that fateful day, which wholly swept me off my feet, and so, equally decided to surprise him with a gift of my virginity because I thought he deserved it. How foolish I was!

When we got back to his hostel later in the evening, I kissed him gratefully while he held me tenderly.

"I hope you enjoyed yourself?" he asked.

"Yeah baby, I really had fun today," I replied him.

Emmanuel was a very tall and heavily built guy who was in his final year

He carried me up, kissed me again for a while, before gently laying me on his bed, and we stared at each other romantically, while my eyes melted as his heavy gaze went all through my body sending shivers down my spine.

"I'm all yours tonight, but please be gentle," I said to him, while he gave me a weird look.

"Are you sure about this?" he asked with an innocent look on his face.

"Yeah, I'm sure, as long as you promise to keep your word that you will never leave me," I replied, while he smiled cheerfully.

"I swear with my life baby, I will never leave you as long as I'm alive," he swore.

"Then I'm all yours sweetheart," I said with a wink, while he smiled. And that was how he had his way with me.

"Please, stop, it's okay," I finally pleaded as I strongly held him, while he gazed into my eyes and jerked as if something had pushed him from behind, before lying on top of me. I closed my eyes as I breathed deeply and gently pushed him away.

"I'm so sorry for hurting you," he apologized as he felt my face with his palms, while I unsuccessfully tried to fight back tears which finally dripped from of my eyes. Why was I crying? I knew not, because I gave him my body willingly and not under duress, but I guess the guilt and feeling of losing my most cherished treasure which I had sworn to keep for my future husband made me cry.

Emmanuel was very caring and comforting as he tried to appease me that night. He boiled water for me, made me tea and even held me all through the night. Truthfully he really was very romantic, which equally increased the love I had for him.

Oh! He simply was an angel that night and I was deceived into believing it was all real. Hmmm, who knew how he must have laughed in his mind that night!

As the whole event played back in my head, I clutched my teddy bear and cried. Even though I had gotten over our break up, I still hadn't gotten over the feeling of losing my virginity to him. How could I have known that it was just a game to him! He had really captured my heart, stolen my soul and swept me off my feet with his charms.

"Dear Lord, I'm now in love again, please, guide me," I prayed even though in my mind I knew my prayer lacked merit.

Emmanuel really was a devil in disguise and after the night I gave him my virginity, he changed from Emmanuel who respected my body, to Mike who loved nothing but sex, and it was as if his eyes opened after our first act which I regretted, and from that moment his attitude towards me changed.

This act then became all he knew and he started demanding for it almost every day which really shocked me. I had thought that after our first time that would be the end of it. I was wrong and it just seemed as if our first act turned him into a sex addict overnight and my foolish self later gave in. I had no option than to oblige him, just to keep my man and prevent him from having external affairs. I just wanted to keep making him happy.

That, really, gave a big blow to my relationship with God. I never had time for school fellowship programs or Christian events on campus again. I was trapped in the relationship that within myself I loosed my prayer life and communion with God. I really felt a huge guilt in me because I willingly gave in to Emmanuel

However, he never did stop caring nor spoiling me with gifts, but then every good deed or affection he showered on me, often ended with him demanding for sex in return and, naively, I continued playing along. He virtually owed my body that period and I couldn't bring myself to disobey him even though sometimes I did try to stop him from having his way with me. This would leave him gloomy for the rest of the day and I would finally give in to his demand just to make him happy.

I wasn't really happy with the way things were going between us, because I knew God wasn't happy with me, but I was just madly in love with this guy, I will say. So there was nothing my weak self could do

"What if something happens and he dumps me?" I often did ask myself that period, but just the thought of it would send cold shivers down my spine, and I would end up saying "GOD FORBID"

He was same time my neighbor that period, which made the closeness unavoidable. Mariam, my best friend, was also not helpful when I finally confided in her, but I really didn't blame her, because she equally wasn't experienced even though she posed like a big girl.

"Is he cheating on you?" she had asked me.

"No," I replied.

"Is he stingy?"

"No."

"Does he hide anything from you?"

"No."

"So what's hard in rewarding him with your body? It's not as if you are losing anything. Moreover you aren't a virgin anymore, and even if you stop having it with him from now till you die, you still won't be a virgin again. Free yourself and enjoy it jor," she had advised, while I stared at her and said nothing.

I kept thinking and pondering on that statement she uttered. She has won my weak self with that, and I agreed with her because the mistake had been done already. Peer influence!

But then the more I gave Emmanuel my body, the bolder he became in demanding for more and it just looked as if he was trying to have it all before graduating, which really scared me. I knew I would still be there for him no matter where he went to, but I guess he didn't trust me and I never knew he had other plans in his mind as he turned me into a love making machine.

It got to a stage where I couldn't take the nonsense act anymore, and surprisingly it led to our first fight.

As these memories flashed back in my mind, my body shook as I sobbed deeply.

The memory was so painful because it was the first time a guy laid his hands on me.

It all happened one fateful evening when we were together in his room; he carried me on his laps and started his foolish act on my foolish self

"Baby you smell nice," he complimented while I blushed, and truthfully Emmanuel was a master of sweet words which he always used on me. That was my greatest weakness.

"What is it baby? Sit up nah," he said as he drew my hand in order for me to sit up but I refused, living him extremely surprised.

"What is the matter?" he asked

"I can't do it," I replied, and he smiled.

He was surprised, he asked why?

"I won't because I don't like it," I said arrogantly, while he stared at me as I got up from his bed and dressed up. His eyes burned furiously as he watched me.

"Baby why are you so selfish?" he finally asked, "What a foolish statement!" I wondered

"You are the one very selfish. All you now know is sex, sex and sex. Just see how skinny you have become" I replied with a hurtful tone. It was really a big mistake and it earned me two powerful resounding slaps on my face. I held my jaw and stared at him in shock and disbelief…OMG!

I stared at him angrily and in shock for a while, before running back to my room in tears.

"Baby I'm sorry," I heard him apologize as he followed me but I shut my door and locked it before he could enter. I was so hurt that day. I never believed Emmanuel could ever lay his hand on me.

Tears flowed freely from my eyes as I remembered how I felt that day. "Why am I even remembering all these?" I asked myself as I cleaned my eyes, but then it was my feeling for Samuel which was bringing my past experience back to my head, and I had no control over it.

Chapter Three

As I lay with my eyes misted with tears, deep in thought, I heard a steady knock on my door, which brought me out from my thoughts. I immediately composed myself as I went to open my door. When I opened it, there stood Samuel with a smile on his gentle face, and he peered into the dark room.

"Are you still sleeping? It's almost 7:45pm," he asked while I forced a smile.

"Actually I wasn't even sleeping," I replied as I yawned, switched on my bulb and allowed him in. He entered, looked around for a while before staring at me again. I tried to hide my face by looking down, but his sharp eyes noticed my dull face and red eyes. Seriously, guys can be very sharp when it comes to reading a girl's face, especially a girl they are interested in.

"What's wrong? What happened?" he asked seriously and with care, while I sat on my bed and looked away. He was soon beside me holding my hands tenderly.

"Please, what is it?" Maybe I can be of help," he asked, while I forced a smile.

"Don't worry it's nothing," I replied, but he just shook his head.

"I don't believe you. Moreover nobody cries over nothing," he insisted.

"Samuel it's nothing serious, I just remembered someone I used to care for," I explained and he smiled.

"Okay, I now understand, so where is he?" he asked but I just gave him a blank look.

"Why do you want to know?" I asked back as I rolled my eyes, which made him smile and shrug. But then my retort didn't put him off, instead he drew closer to me and looked into my eyes.

"Sweetheart, a problem shared is a problem half solved. Sharing your story with a friend sometimes helps to reduce tension and bad feelings. I also promise to share my story with you when you are done with yours," he said to me fearlessly, while I looked at him silently as I battled within my mind whether to share my secret with him or not. I thought to myself that no matter my feelings for him, he still is a boy and might use it against me in future, but the way he stared at me really showed he cared, and the sparkles in his eyes were very real and filled with love. My eyes melted again and I burst into tears while he held me in his arms and consoled me.

"It is okay baby," he said with his gentle voice. Truthfully, I didn't know how I felt that moment because it had been a long time a guy held me in that manner.

His arms were comforting and I really felt like sleeping in them when he held me, but then I didn't want to appear vulnerable or weak to him and so I managed to control and keep myself in check by drying my eyes.

"It's okay everything happens for a purpose." "What are you going to eat tonight?" he added, while I said nothing.

"I have soup, I can make Garri for you," he said, which made me laugh.

"Thanks Sam. You are a nice guy but don't worry, I will drink tea with my biscuit," I replied, while he shrugged in resignation.

"Don't worry once I'm done with my night bath I will come and spend an hour with you," I had said to him, when I finally composed myself and stopped my tears that evening. He stared at me as if he was reading my mind through my eyes.

"Do you promise? Because I can't wait to hear your story?" he asked, while I smiled and nodded.

"Yeah, I promise," I replied, before he stood up and left in order to give me space to take my bath.

As it is of common knowledge, we girls like to keep our secrets to ourselves but then Samuel appeared very special to me, because he had few friends and didn't socialize much. This made me to trust him with my secret. The way I felt for Samuel was such that I sometimes felt I was charmed. Yet, I couldn't help it and at precisely 8:55pm that evening I was in his room where we stared at each other as if we were searching for something in our eyes.

After taking my night bath that evening, I took my biscuit and a cup of tea to his room as I had promised.

"So dear, I'm all ears," he said to me with a smile, while I drank my tea and smiled back as I prepared to share my story with him.

And there I sat in his room about to reveal my intimate secrets to a male who really was nothing but a stranger to me. With a smile on my face I opened my mouth to do what I never knew I would ever do in my life.

Hmmm, love really works wonders.

I told him the first few chapters of my love life with Emmanuel, which was focused on how we started and how he took away my virginity, and subsequently turned into a satyriasist. Frankly, I knew not what pushed me into revealing some part of my intimate life to him, even though I kept the main part to myself. While I narrated my sad story, he listened keenly with his eyes focused on me.

"So how did it all end?" he seriously asked, while I sighed heavily. I stopped my story at the scene where Emmanuel slapped me. My face glowed as I noticed the excitement with which he asked the last question.

"I will say our affair officially ended on his graduation day," I replied, as the memory of that particular day rushed into my head, while Samuel nodded his head for me to continue.

Then I continued.

Emmanuel's graduation day really was a day I will never forget in a hurry. That night was really spectacular, as we made love all through in celebration of good things to come. At least, so I thought. But I was celebrating the beginning of the end of our relationship.

That particular day was a very great and special day for Emmanuel, and his happiness knew no bounds.

After settling the hostel neighbors by giving them a carton of malt and beer to share, he dragged me out from the hostel happily.

"Dear, it's you and I today, let's go catch some fun," he whispered into my ear, while I giggled happily. Foolish me!

He took me to a small fast food joint at the other end of the town, where he spoiled me silly with chicken pepper soup and ice cream, together with sweet romantic words which followed it.

It was one of the best romantic moments I ever had with him and I was the happiest girl on earth that fateful day. When we got back to his room around 8pm in the evening, he held me tenderly.

"Baby thanks a lot for being by my side all through my struggle as a student," he whispered, while my eyes melted. Oh, I was so much in love with him as I prepared myself to give him my body once again.

"Dear, please continue," I heard Samuel say to me, while I stared back at him with a smile on my face.

"Sometimes a little girl needs to keep some stories to herself," I said and winked at him, while he shifted unhappily where he sat.

"It isn't fair oo," he protested, making me smile further.

"I'm very sorry but I can't continue," I apologized, as I reached for his hand which I held softly.

Truthfully, I couldn't really bring myself to share the rest of my story with him, because a girl really needs to keep some secrets to herself.

"I think it's time to get going," I said to Samuel who just looked at me unhappily.

"You are not keeping your promise. It's not what we agreed," he continued to protest while I stood up.

"Don't worry in due time you will know everything," I said to him, while he shrugged.

"I don't have a choice, so let me just wait patiently and hopefully," he said to me, while I laughed, picked my tea cup and left for my room.

I rinsed my tea cup when I got to my room before lying down to sleep, but still sleep eluded me once again, as the memory of my last moments with Emmanuel flashed back into my head.

His goodbye really was the most sincere words he ever spoke to me and equally the saddest words I ever heard, but then I misinterpreted his goodbye thinking that it was just a normal parting word of a travelling boyfriend, without knowing that it was a final goodbye from a guy abandoning his girlfriend and walking out from a relationship which she jealously guided with her whole heart.

***

After his final exams, he had only stayed for two weeks before packing up some of his properties, even though his rent was not yet due. My heart skipped countless times as I helped him pack his things, something I did out of loyalty and not because I wanted him to leave.

"Why are you leaving so soon, how about your clearance?" I had asked, while he just smiled as he held me.

"Don't worry dear, they have all been taken care of and I'm just leaving because I don't want to waste any time in preparing the road for our future," he replied sweetly, while I stared at him with a fast beating heart filled with love.

"I'm very scared," I said to him, while he smiled before kissing me passionately.

"You have nothing to fear princess. I can never forget your beauty or the love we share. Just trust me. In fact I should really be the one to be scared, because you are too beautiful to be left alone," I heard him say, while I blushed. His sweet words were too much for my inexperienced little brain, and his lips rested on mine again.

He had control over me again at that point that I was just a toy in his hands and even when we quarreled I forgave him easily even when I swore not to.

As we made love once again, I didn't know it was a goodbye gift from him. All I did was just to enjoy every bit of it with no knowledge that I was being dumped.

As soon as Emmanuel packed and left the hostel, I felt very empty. It looked as though I had lost something precious. I had gotten used to his presence. I couldn't even stay five minutes without thinking about him, or stay an hour without flashing or calling his phone.

It really appeared as if my whole life depended on him and that was exactly when I started to notice some changes in him.

His phone calls drastically reduced to the extent of twice on a very good week. I really didn't care about that since I did most of the calling. Then the saddest thing happened when he didn't call me on my birthday but only sent a text message. It got me extremely annoyed and terribly shocked.

"How can a text message be compared to his sweet voice?" I had asked myself throughout that day as I waited patiently for his phone call which never came. Yet with tears in my eyes I read his text message over and over again until I eventually fell asleep.

"Was he waiting for me to call him on my own birthday?" I wondered sorrowfully.

It was very disheartening to receive phone calls from friends who meant nothing to me, while the person I called my boyfriend found it very hard to call me "Did I truly choose the right person?" I asked myself over and over again that night.

I didn't expect him to buy me jewels or clothes, because I knew he just graduated. All I yearned for was to hear his voice that particular day, but it was rather too difficult a thing for him to do.

I couldn't control my emotions the following day and with trembling hands, I dialed his phone number.

"Hey baby, what's up?" he asked when he picked his phone, but due to my anger I couldn't answer him, but instead poured out my unhappiness to him.

"You have really changed! You can't even call me on my birthday. You are very heartless; please don't call my number again!"

I poured out to him before ending the call. Even though I shouted at him, I had expected him to call me back. So I held my phone hopefully, thinking he would call back, but my hope faded when seconds passed into minutes and minutes to hours, yet his call didn't come. I can't describe how I felt that moment, because I was more than devastated. He finally called me around 9pm, but due to my anger which had then built up to the brim, I refused to answer my phone which rang five times before a text message came in.

The text message was from him and when I read it, I almost collapsed.

"I knew it will come to this one day but I never expected it could be this soon. Anyway, good luck with your life. I know you are with another guy that's why you are not answering your phone. I won't disturb you again just as you ordered."

The text message he sent smote my heart and tears dropped freely from my eyes as I read it over and over again hoping it read different.

"So Emmanuel had never trusted me," I said to myself as I cried and the urge to call him back and beg him that moment was so great, that I had to drop my phone.

"Life why are you this cruel?" I heard myself ask. Mariam my roommate rushed to my side with concern written all over her face but I said nothing as I handed my phone to her. Her face equally turned white as she read the text message Emmanuel sent me.

"Hmmm, so cruel," I said to myself as all the memories kept flashing back.

"Baby girl, this text message shouldn't depress you. I believe he is just angry, you know how guys behave sometimes," Mariam tried to console me but yet I was unable to stop myself from crying that night.

The following morning, she called him with her own phone but he refused to answer. It really surprised Mariam and all she did was just shrug and shake her head in disbelief.

"Don't get yourself worked up over him. He should be the person to cry for you. So dear, let's forget about him and prepare for market. You know our food stuffs have finished," she said to me as she expertly changed the topic.

Emmanuel never called me, neither did I see him for the rest of that year but I soon pushed him behind my mind as I focused all my energy in my studies, the reason I came to school in the first place. I wasn't in school to fall in love with someone who didn't even deserve me.

However, that period was very traumatic for me, because I woke up some days feeling very lonely. What actually kept me going was my determination to get over him as I swore not to be so easily used again. I couldn't believe that a guy like Emmanuel, who met me when I was very pure, could easily forget me, as though I never existed. This, as well, steeled my heart towards guys such that most of them avoided me because of my cold attitude towards them.

It was also my past with Emmanuel that made me pack out from my former hostel and move into the hostel where I met Samuel.

Chapter Four

Hmmm, Samuel! The guy who softened me a bit and made my heart beat fast again.

"I hope I'm not making a major mistake again?" I asked myself as I tossed around on my bed. I honestly didn't know how his charms were able to soften my heart and turn me back to a sweet girl capable of loving again.

I was still thinking about him when my phone rang briefly and stopped. When I checked the caller, it was no other person but Samuel who had given me a drop call. A smile appeared on my face. I checked the time and it was 12:15am.

"Why is he awake by this time of the night? Is he thinking about me?" I asked myself with a smile. I was still pondering over it when sleep finally carried me away.

Oh my Samuel…

***

"I like Samuel very much, but I'm scared of making another mistake," I confessed to Mariam, on our way to our hostel from school the following day, while she just smiled.

"Sometimes I don't understand you," I heard her say, which made me stare at her in surprise.

"What do you mean?" I asked,

"Nothing jare," she replied, which only made me more curious to know what she had in mind.

"Nawa for you, tell me what you have in mind nah?" I insisted, adding some Pidgin English. She stared at me for a while with a very serious look on her face.

"Your problem with Emmanuel happened last year. What I don't understand is why you are still mourning him, and as well punishing yourself to this moment," she said, which shocked me immensely.

"Who told you I'm still mourning Emma or punishing myself?" I asked seriously.

"Isn't it obvious that you are? It's been months since you last had a guy in your life. Which kind of punishment is more than that?" she fired back.

"Abeg oo, it's no punishment to me, I'm single and happy," I replied with a smile, while she laughed for a while.

"Comot there jare! Pretender, don't tell me that crap again jor," she said with laughter, again, adding Pidgin English, while I eyed her.

One thing I really did love about my friend Mariam was her honest and blunt nature. She also never hid her feelings from me, even for a single day.

"If you like, continue to play hide and seek with that poor boy's feelings. I have nothing else to tell you again," she added, while I slapped her shoulder,

"Madam, it's okay nah," I replied her.

***

Falling in love for the second time isn't that easy, especially when you have been so terribly dealt with, the first time, but then love is an inevitable force of attraction which does come to every human being, and when it comes, carries your whole body, soul and even sense of reasoning with it.

Truly I was so scared of being hurt again, because I knew I barely managed to survive my first heartbreak. I didn't know how my friends, especially Mariam, were able to jump from one relationship to another without any emotional breakdown.

"How I wish I could just be like them," I had often said, but then I really couldn't be like them, because we weren't the same.

We soon got to our hostel. Mariam gave me a sweet smile before going to her own room which she shared with her boyfriend.

"Take care, I will come to your room later," she said as she smiled.

As I stood before my door searching through by handbag to get my keys, Samuel came out from his own room, with a sweet smile on his face.

"Finally you are back. I have been lonely all day," he said as he walked towards me, while I stared at him with a smile. I felt like hugging him that moment as my body yearned for his arms around me. I however kept myself in check, and swallowed my wishes because I knew he had no morale to hug me in that manner in a hostel corridor.

But surprisingly, he drew close and hugged me, which really drew out dimples from my face.

"I couldn't sleep last night because I was thinking about us," I heard him whisper

Hmmm, love is full of surprises!

We walked into my room together, where he sat quietly on my bed and watched as I quickly prepared rice that afternoon. I had returned from school very hungry. The way he stared at me that afternoon really made me lose concentration a couple of times and also made me uncomfortable.

"Please stop staring at me nah," I finally muttered while he laughed.

"But I can't stop myself from staring at you nah," he replied mimicking my tone, making me sigh with a smile.

"You better go back to your room and watch your TV since you are looking for whom to watch," I fired back while he laughed out loud.

"Watching you cook is more interesting than any TV program," he joked while I eyed him.

"Big head," I cursed

"Flat nyash," he cursed back.

"Na there your eyes go see fast," I replied, while he fell on the bed as he laughed.

"Madam, cook fast, I'm very hungry," he said as he laughed.

"I'm not your mother," I replied, as I eyed him.

After cooking, I freshened up in my bathroom, before dishing out the rice I cooked on a large plate. We ate together in silence and the way he ate told me that he was actually hungry.

"You cook nice, but my Mum cook's better," he finally joked, breaking the silence that had ensued for some time.

"Because you don fill your stomach nah. Why didn't you make that comment earlier?" I asked with an angry mien, while he smiled.

"I hope there is still some left in the pot?" he also asked,

"Why are you asking?" I asked back with a feigned frown,

"Because I will still eat at night nah," he replied, while I sighed with a smile. Seriously that boy's head needed to be spanked that moment.

We were soon in his room where we joked and laughed as we watched a movie. I was very glad that he finally was able to feel at ease with me.

Then he made a statement which shocked me.

"This is my first time of being this close to a girl," he confessed as he swallowed hard, while I stared at him in silence and surprise. I totally knew not how to react or what to say, but then his eyes really said it all as he looked into mine.

"So Samuel is actually a virgin. How I wish I had kept mine till now also," I said to myself as I stared back at him with a fast beating heart.

"I hope my confession hasn't changed anything?" I heard Samuel anxiously ask, while I touched his jaw and smiled,

"No dear, it hasn't," I replied sweetly, and he heaved a sigh of relief, before giving me a kiss on my cheek.

I truly didn't know what else to tell him, and so I stared silently at him. I guess he noticed that I had gone out of what to say as he drew closer and whispered into my right ear…

"I hope you are alright baby, because you are yet to make any comment." I breathed deeply, but still, no word could come out.

"I know you are very surprised," he said as he held my right hand. I nodded and smiled,

"Sure I am, because it is very hard to believe that at your age and level you have never been intimate with a woman, even for once," I replied, and he looked down with a drawn face.

"I know something caused it and I can read it in your eyes and expression. Tell me what it is," I curiously inquired, but he just fidgeted and looked away.

"Open up to me Sam, you will gain my trust more by opening up" I added, while he bit his lips and stared at me painfully.

"I dated a girl for four years without making love to her," he confessed and looked down in shame and pain. I reached out my hand and drew his face up, and into his eyes I gazed,

"Tell me how it all happened dear?" I asked curiously, with a fast beating heart, while he shook his head.

"I loved her with my whole body, soul and spirit, but she took all in her hands and crushed as if it was nothing," he said sorrowfully, while I firmly held his hand as I listened to him.

"So tell me about her," I gently urged, and he swallowed hard and bit his lips.

"We started dating from our last year in High School. She was in same class with me and coincidentally we got admitted into this University the same year. All went well

29

at first, even though we never made love. She said we should save it for marriage which I also supported, since I loved and trusted her with all my heart. Moreover she posed as a good Christian, so I had no doubt over her intentions or fidelity. Sadly, everything came crashing last year, when she started to hang out with a boy she introduced to me as her course mate. Before I knew what was happening she finally told me she didn't have feelings for me anymore," he narrated sadly, while my heart wept for him.

I drew his hands and embraced him, while he tightly held me like a child clinging unto its mother.

"Oh Samuel, only if you haven't been so dull, this wouldn't have happened to you," I said to myself as we held each other. My love for him equally doubled, because I also deserved to have a male virgin for myself.

Can two broken hearts linked together create an indestructible bond of love?

He tried to kiss me again, but I politely pushed his face away, and his expression changed as he looked at me curiously,

"I hope I no fall hands to confess to you?" he anxiously asked in Pidgin English, while I bursted into laughter,

"No dear you didn't," I answered amidst laughter. He kept quiet and just watched me.

"It's just that I have to get going, because I have a school assignment I wish to attend to this evening," I explained, while he shrugged.

"Okay, but I do feel you are running away from me," he replied, and I breathed deeply,

"Dear, I will return once I'm done with my assignment," I assured him, while he shrugged again.

"It's okay, and also remember to bring another plate of rice when coming," he added. I then got up with a smile and left his room.

I truly had no assignment to do that evening, but only wanted to be alone for a moment in order to control and put myself together. I didn't want to be betrayed by my excitement. Moreover his confession really overwhelmed me, because I never dreamt I'd be so lucky to have a male virgin, whom I liked so much for myself.

"Hmmm, am I not a lucky girl?" I asked my image as I stared at my mirror with a smile.

I was still admiring myself from the mirror when I heard a knock on my door.

I opened my door happily expecting to see Mariam, my best friend who had promised to show up, but my smile quickly disappeared when I saw David standing at the door way.

"Hello pretty girl, I came to keep you company," he said with a smile as he walked into my room, without even waiting for me to admit him in. I froze in fear because everyone knew him as a notorious cultist.

David was a very handsome and rich guy. However, he ruined himself by belonging to a cult group, and was so into it that he was very popular within and outside the hostel and school environment. He actually felt like the world only revolved around money and cultism.

As he sat on my bed with a smile, I wondered what really brought him to my room by that time of the day.

He crossed his leg as he stared at me with a confident smile, while I sat on my plastic chair and faced him with a drawn face. Even though I was scared, I never showed it.

"Are you not happy that I came to your room?" I heard him ask, while I shook my head and forced out a smile.

"I'm not feeling fine, and I was even about to sleep before you knocked," I replied.

"But I just saw you coming out from Samuel's room minutes ago" he said. I just kept quiet and held my jaw with both hands.

"But on a serious note why is a pretty girl like you always hanging out with someone with no 'swag'?" he asked with a serious look on his face. I breathed deeply as I stared into his eyes with disgust.

"I like boys with no swag," I replied, in a manner which would even make a brave 'Jew student' raise his eye brow in fear, but I cared not, because I really didn't like even the air he breathed.

"Baby we are not quarreling nah? Please I'm also your friend," he said calmly, while I shifted uneasily on my chair,

"I'm so sorry for the tone I used, it's just that I need to rest, please," I said to him, while he shrugged, stood up, and came to my side.

"Okay dear, I will check on you tomorrow. Please do take care of yourself," he said to me as he caressed my hair a bit while I held my breath. I strongly withheld myself from making any annoying comment. His touch was very irritating, but not as much as I detested his composure. He just behaved confidently as though he owned both I and the hostel.

He finally left my room with a well composed smile which really annoyed me more, but I soon forgot all about him as I rested for a while before warming my rice and dishing out some for Samuel as promised.

However, as I stepped out from my room with a plate of rice around 9:00pm, I ran into him again as he was coming out from the hostel balcony, and he smiled as he saw me.

"Mary, seems like you are now okay?" he asked, jovially, while I smiled and walked pass him.

Samuel was very happy when I brought the rice for him, and he thanked me countless times as he devoured it. While he ate, I smiled confidently as I watched him.

I didn't tell him about David's visit. It appeared very irrelevant to be discussed at that time. A part of me urged me to tell him but I suppressed and kept it to myself, even though I didn't know whether I did the right thing, especially with the events which later unfolded.

"Please can you sleep in my room tonight?" I heard myself ask Samuel, who froze for a while as he stared at me in surprise. I honestly didn't know what pushed me to make such a request. I guess it was because I was scared of David and what he could do, which really didn't make a whole lot of sense. Somehow, I knew within me that I secretly wish to spend the night with Samuel.

However, I also knew what I did when I made such demand because as a girl it would have been easier for me to sleep in his room, but because of my pride I had rephrased my demand, which I thought any sharp guy would understand the hidden meaning.

Samuel was at lost on what to say. He just stared at me for a while before he was able to find his voice.

"Is everything okay?" he asked with concern, while I just nodded.

"Yeah, it's just that I'm having a bad feeling which is making me scared," I replied.

"Don't worry dear, I will be by your side tonight," he assured me with a smile, while I smiled in appreciation, even though I was disappointed that he didn't insist for me to sleep in his room.

However, nothing really happened that night in my room, even though we both lay awake till very late in the night. I was awake because it was my first time of spending the night with another boy since I broke up with my Ex-boyfriend. I easily noticed that Samuel was also awake because he kept tossing around on my bed. I didn't know whether it was because he was uncomfortable in my room that made him toss around or because he was summoning the courage to touch me.

He finally drew close and held me. It delighted me so much, but I kept quiet and pretended to be asleep. To my greatest dismay he didn't go further or do anything else to me before we finally slept.

After that night, my respect for him grew, because he behaved like a real gentleman whom he had always claimed to be.

We woke up very late the following morning to a steady knock on my door. I was forced to open my door when the person knocking refused to give up.

It was precisely 7:05AM when I opened my door that morning, to see David standing on my door-way, with hands in his pocket, and a fixed smile on his face.

What is his plan?

Did he get to know that Samuel and I slept together?

I instantly broke free from David when I saw Samuel enter my room. My heart furiously pounded while my legs shook as he sat on my bed with a blank expression.

David just stood with a smile on his face as he stared at Samuel, who pretended as if he didn't notice his presence.

"My guy how far nah," I heard David say, as he drew close to him with an extended right hand, which he unhappily shook with a dry smile on his face. I felt like disappearing like a ghost as I watched them with frightened eyes.

"Baby I have to get going; we will continue our discussion later, okay!" David said with a smile before leaving my room, while all I did was just to stare at him silently. I was extremely confused that moment.

"Here are the movies you asked me to buy," Samuel said coldly, as he stood up with a nylon bag, immediately after David left. I drew closer to him and stared into his eyes, but he instantly looked away.

He dropped the small plastic bag, which instantly opened as soon as it landed on my bed, revealing a cup of ice cream, a well wrapped cake and two DVD plates, which I eyed hungrily on seeing.

"I'm going to my room, do have a nice evening," he added with a cold tone, which sent cold shivers down my spine. I instantly reached for his right hand, which I held tightly with trembling hands.

"Why are you leaving so soon and why is your voice so cold?" I asked, even though I knew the reason he was angry, but naturally as a girl I pretended not to know. Moreover, I actually owed him no explanation, because I wasn't yet officially his girlfriend.

"Please, I'm very tired, we will talk later," he replied, without even looking at me. I bit my lips as I cursed David in my mind.

"What you saw earlier is not exactly what it looked like. He just forced himself on me," I tried to explain with a whole lot of courage. I hated explaining my actions to anyone. I had to do it because I truly cared about him. But my explanation only made him angrier, and his eyes furiously burned as he looked up at me in a way I never had seen him look.

"Let me go. You girls are all the same," he muttered, snatched his hand from my grip and left my room. His last words smote my heart like a double edged sword.

Oh how it pains to be wrongfully accused or suspected.

I battled with my pride as I watched him leave. Truly I felt like following him to his room that moment and continue with my explanation, but I held myself.

"Let him be for now. Don't go after him, you are a girl for Christ's sake," my mind advised.

I locked my door and lay on my bed, while my thoughts kept me company as I wondered and reasoned how Samuel must have felt when he saw David and me hugging.

"But it was just a friendly hug," I reassured myself and sighed.

I was confused on how to approach Samuel or apologize to him without appearing cheap. There was nothing I hated more than a girl begging a guy over anything.

"I did that as a little naive girl. I don't think I will stoop so low for him," I muttered to myself, even though my mind wasn't as strong as I sounded.

Two hours later, I left my room and knocked on his door which opened a minute later. It however wasn't Samuel who opened the door, but one of David's friends who was also our neighbor.

I gasped in surprise when I saw him, because I knew he wasn't friendly or close with Samuel, but I kept my thoughts to myself, as I forced out a smile and entered into the room.

I panicked and shook in fear when I also saw David sitting on a plastic chair with a smile on his face, while Samuel sat on his rug and faced his television. I smelt danger immediately, even though everything appeared normal inside the room.

"Hahaha, your friend is already here, we have to get going," David said with a smile as he nodded to his friend, who was at the door, stood up and shook hands with Samuel.

"Don't look at me that way nah, I just came to see Sam and also make him my friend. You know he hardly talks to people," He explained as he drew close and touched my left cheek, before leaving the room with his friend.

"I hope everything is okay?" I asked Samuel with concern, immediately we were alone but he said nothing to me.

"Talk to me, please," I anxiously pleaded as I held his left hand.

"Everything is fine," he said with a dry smile, while I shook my head.

"Your voice doesn't sound alright; tell me what did he say to you?" I asked, but he just smiled again and stared at me.

"It's just boy's talk and nothing you should know," he replied coldly, before facing his TV again. I bit my lips, stormed out from his room, and marched towards David's room angrily.

I never knew I had such courage to march towards David's room that evening unaided. I soon got to his door and knocked furiously. But I was caught off guard when a pretty slim girl opened the door and stared at me in surprise.

"Eemm is David inside?" I managed to ask, but the girl just kept quiet and looked me over. Luckily David soon appeared with a smile behind the girl.

"I know you will surely show up. Linda, make way for our visitor to enter nah," I heard him say.

"I didn't come for a friendly visit. Please, leave Samuel and I alone. We didn't do anything to you," I barked at him furiously, while his smile quickly died away, as my words hit him like a disfigured 504 salon car.

Linda equally stared at me with confusion in her eyes, while David quickly controlled his surprise and forced out a smile again.

"Come inside lets discuss, I don't understand your outburst," he said to me, but I just eyed him furiously and walked away fearlessly.

'Imagine, the idiot even has a girl in his room. Tomorrow he will claim that she is his sister, mtcheeew," I said with a long hiss as I walked back to Samuel's room.

"Where did you go to?" he anxiously asked, as soon as I entered his room.

"I went to give that silly David a piece of my mind," I replied, while his face coloured immediately.

"Are you crazy? What did you just do?" he asked with a slightly raised tone, while my eyes equally sparkled with anger as I stared at him.

"You asked whether I'm crazy, right? No problem, I brought all these problems and insults upon myself," I said angrily, stood up and left his room.

"No. Wait I never meant to insult you," I heard him plead, as he rushed up and held my left hand. I snatched it from him and walked to my room.

He knocked on my door for hours, called my phone countless times, and even sent me lots of text messages that evening but I ignored all of them. I really wanted to punish him a little and of course I enjoyed every bit of it.

I also heard David's pattern of knocking on my door later in the night but also ignored it and slept away.

Early the next day, I went downstairs with my bucket to fetch water. I had planned to travel home that day.

"Hello," I heard a feminine voice greet me as I was filling my bucket with tap water. I turned instantly with a smile, and there stood the same girl I saw in David's room the previous day, staring at me.

"What's up dear," I replied politely,

"Do you recognize me?" she asked,

"Of course I do. Were you not the girl in David's room yesterday?" I replied and asked,

"Yeah I'm the girl, I'm so sorry for being a little rude to you yesterday," she apologized, while I laughed,

"Were you rude to me? Hmmm I didn't even notice it. Anyway, it's cool my name is Mary," I said to her.

"Thanks dear. Mine is Linda," she replied.

"Yeah I know," I said with a smile as I carried my bucket, while she blushed.

"Please there is something I wish to sit down and discuss with you," she humbly pleaded. I stared at her in surprise and breathed deeply.

"I'm travelling today, but I'll be back by tomorrow afternoon. Will tomorrow evening be okay for you?" I asked,

"Yeah it will, I will come over to your room," she replied with glittering eyes, which made her look even more beautiful.

"Do you know my room?" I asked with surprise,

"Of course I do," she replied with a smile,

"Okay till then," I said as I nodded in agreement before walking away with my bucket of water, wondering what she wanted to discuss with me.

I really couldn't relax when I finally travelled home that day as I kept wondering what Linda wanted to discuss with me, but then I had choice than to have patience till the next evening when we scheduled our meeting for.

***

"I don't understand you anymore, are you still angry with me?" I heard Samuel asked as I finally answered his phone

41

call later in the evening. Truly I was so glad to hear his voice. Even though I was angry with him for the tone and words he used on me the previous day, I knew I was also at fault.

"Let's just forget about it, it's all in the past," I replied calmly,

"Thank God you know. Anyway, where are you?" he asked,

"I travelled home but I will be back tomorrow," I replied,

"Oh my God! See your way nah, you just travelled without informing me?" he accused bitterly,

"I'm sorry, though you caused it," I muttered quietly.

I returned the next day with a heavy pocket and lots of foodstuffs which gladdened my heart.

"God bless you mummy," I sang to myself.

After I had kept all my foodstuffs in their locations, I freshened up and headed to Samuel's room, dressed in my black sleeveless top and a short. With a bowl of oranges, guava and English pear in my left hand, I knocked on his door which opened seconds later.

"Oh goodness me!" he exclaimed immediately his eyes fell on me. I smiled and cat-walked into his room.

"Did you miss me?" I asked with a smile.

"Of course I missed you," he replied instantly as he stared at me with a surprising look.

"Here are the fruits I brought for you. I hope you know how to peel oranges?" I asked with a smile, as I stood up seconds later.

"No I don't know how to peel them," he replied jokingly.

"I will peel them for you later in the evening. I want to go and prepare soup with the ingredients my Mum gave me before they get spoilt," I explained, while he breathed deeply.

"Okay then let's go together," he said with a smile.

"No, don't bother I'm expecting a friend," I replied. He bit his lips and stared at me suspiciously, but luckily for him, he didn't ask any stupid question which could have brought another problem between us.

"Okay then. I guess I'll have to wait here for the soup," he said with a forced smile.

"I never said I was bringing any for you," I joked, touched his jaw and left without another word.

I really do love to cook. It is one of the qualities I inherited from my Mum who never gets tired of cooking even when her children are around.

I was soon done with the soup, and as I was about bringing it down from my Stove, I heard gentle knocks on my door.

The airs were gentle. The sharp rays of the setting sun which gave beauty to the evening penetrated my windows into my room, meeting me where I had sat on a plastic chair relaxing.

Just as I left the spot to find refuge in my bed, I heard a gentle knock on my door.

"Hey dear, I hope I came at the right time?" Linda asked sweetly as I got my door a minute later.

"Yeah dear, in fact you came at the right time. I just finished cooking a pot of soup," I replied with a lovely smile.

"Really! I thought you just returned?" she asked, while I just smiled and shrugged,

"Kpom kpom kpommm kpom kpom kpom kpom!" David's pattern of knocking soon sounded on my door, moments later as we were about settling down for discussion.

"Who could be knocking this way?" I heard Linda ask,

"I think it's David," I answered with a smile as I watched her face, while she instantly gasped in fear.

"Please I don't want him to know I'm here," Linda held my left hand and pleaded with frightened eyes, while I looked at her in surprise as I equally searched her face.

"I will explain later but please don't let him come into your room," she added, trembling.

"Don't worry dear, I won't," I assured her with a smile.

I finally opened my door half way with a fast beating heart, and blocked the entrance with my body as I stared at David, who just smiled sweetly at me like an innocent child.

"Hey dear, how you dey?" he asked,

"I'm fine but just busy with my assignments," I replied,

"Can I come in? I promise not to disturb you, I'm very bored and lonely in my room," he asked with a smile, while I shook my head.

"Can you please come some other time? I really want to be alone," I answered with a serious look. He smiled, shrugged and gave me a cold look which really frightened me.

"Okay, I will come later in the evening," he said before walking away, while I breathed deeply.

"What is wrong with this boy?" I asked myself.

"Has he gone?" Linda inquired curiously as soon as I locked my door, while I smiled and advanced towards her.

"Yes dear, he has gone back to where he came from," I replied with a smile, while she breathed deeply.

"Thank God," I heard her mutter.

"So dear I'm very eager to hear what you came to discuss with me," I said curiously as I sat beside her, but she just looked away as if she wasn't sure of herself any more.

"I have a feeling David knows I'm here," I heard her mutter with a lost voice. I drew closer and rested my right hand on her left shoulder,

"What is really going on and why are you so scared of him?" I asked,

"I don't think it's important anymore I have to get going," she said and stood up suddenly, while I held her left hand strongly, and pleaded with her.

"Please open up to me. I promise to keep our discussion secret," I pleaded desperately, even though I really didn't know what pushed me to do so.

She stared at me silently for a while before sitting back on the bed.

"I can't help but notice how attached and obsessed David has become over you. Do you have feelings for him?" she asked as she looked into my eyes, while I instantly was thrown into shock, confusion and surprise. I really didn't know the motive behind her question, whether she asked it as a girlfriend, sister, solicitor or a jealous stalker. But before I could get my composure back, her phone rang.

Her face coloured as she stared at her ringing phone for a while before standing up again.

"I better start going, we will talk some other time," she muttered as she walked towards the door, while I stared at her in silence. I was extremely surprised and confused.

She left my room without another word, while I stood up, walked to my closed door, locked it and returned to my bed, where I lay with my thoughts before falling asleep.

***

I jolted from my bed around 7:30pm that evening, prepared my night meal, freshened up, and left for Samuel's room. I walked into his room with a tray of Garri and soup, while he stared at me happily when he opened his door.

"I thought you weren't coming again," he confessed.

"I was carried away by sleep," I explained with a yawn,

"And where did it drop you?" he asked as he brought a bowl of water,

"It dropped me on your head," I joked. He laughed and washed his hands.

We ate silently because we were very hungry, and he also never asked about the friend whom I told him I was expecting earlier in the day, earning him a great deal of my respect, even though I knew I wouldn't have been able to hold myself from asking, if I was in his shoes.

We were soon done with the meal, and he then sat by my side and waited upon me as I peeled oranges for him.

"You don't know how much you have changed my life and the kind of influence you now have over me," he muttered moments later, while I blushed.

"Seriously, dear, you have redefined my life and I do owe you a lot for that. I know I'm not romantic, but I'm trying my best to learn, I promise to do everything within my power to make you happy. I love you so much," he poured out to me, while my hands shook slightly.

He reached for the orange I held with my left hand, took it from my grasp, knelt by my side and gave me a warm hug.

I trembled under the hotness of his tight hug and it was as if a thousand volts of love had hit me. He drew up my face and stared into my eyes,

"Oh baby, I wish you could feel how my heart is beating for you," he muttered,

"I wish you could feel how I'm trembling inside because of you," I said to myself.

I actually wished for something more lovely than the regular hug, but it never seemed close. This made a part of me happy and another sad but still didn't change my feelings for him.

"I think I'm in love with a saint here," I said to myself.

Our love affair grew stronger from that day, and we could have dated happily ever after if not for David who often showed up to mess things up. He continued wooing me and nothing I did to stop him seemed to have any effect on him, instead it appeared to make him more desperate than ever. It truly alarmed me that I had no choice than to seek Mariam's advice and help who then suggested that we teamed up with Linda before confronting him.

Against Samuel's approval, I accepted Mariam's suggestion and tried to reach an agreement with Linda, but my first attempt failed when David mysteriously showed up and ruined the whole thing by expressing his feelings to me in Linda's presence, suddenly making her more jealous and suspicious that I had to flee from her room that evening.

I truly was very hurt and beaten by David's unexpected cunning move that I utterly decided to give up, but, no, Mariam wouldn't accept defeat and urged me to go back and explain things to Linda, which I did with her by my side.

When we were about gaining Linda's confidence again, David appeared as usual from nowhere to mess things again for us, even though he came this time with two other bad boys who blocked and locked us inside Linda's room. Only God knew his plan that day.

A bitter argument instantly ensued between David and Linda which soon resulted to David rendering her a sharp slap. A visibly provoked and angry Mariam instantly jumped up to Linda's defense and dared David.

In the confrontation and exchange of words that followed, David finally revealed to Mariam that he wasn't going to touch her only because her boyfriend was a member of his gang. This instantly stunned Mariam and left her speechless.

I had to intervene by calling him a liar, but before he could reply my comment, Linda angrily attacked him with a kitchen knife. Luckily enough, he saw her on time, side stepped and tried to grab the knife, but he miscalculated, and screamed as the sharp blade cut his last left finger.

We all gasped.

David stared at his injured finger for a while before descending heavily on Linda, kicking, hitting and slapping her randomly with fury.

Linda's cry soon shook the whole lodge, making us freeze like statues as she received David's blows all alone. I truly had never heard or witnessed anyone cry with such pain and anguish before in my life, but instead of rendering any help, I just stood and watched as if I was watching a home video.

Perhaps it was because my strength failed me that moment or because I was too scared to jump into the fight.

Whatever it was that prevented me from intervening that moment, turned me into a very heartless girl who just stood and watched a fellow girl as she got beaten in a fight which truly started because she happened to be in that room that moment.

"Supposing Mariam and I left things as they were all these wouldn't have happened but I guess it's now too late to be regretting," I reasoned as I watched him beat up Linda.

Mariam was still too stunned to intervene, as she sat speechless on the bed with both hands on her head.

After David's revelation about her boyfriend that evening, she just coloured up and kept to herself like an AIDS patient.

Finally, I heaved a sigh of relief with a deep breath as David's two friends rushed up and dragged him out from Linda, who just lay motionless from the terrifying blows she got from him. The poor girl really had given up with her struggles when her strength failed her, yet David really was very furious to care or even notice.

Supposing his two friends didn't break him away from her that moment, I truly didn't know what would have happened.

David and his friends finally left us alone in 'pieces' and I was then left with the huge task of reviving Linda. Poor Linda was trampled upon, humiliated and beaten all because of love.

With shaking hands, I lifted up her head and tried to revive her.

Where's this going to end?

How do I end David's case all at once?

"David is a devil," Linda cried as I helped her sit up,

"I will report him to school security and the police," I assured her,

"No, don't do that, it will only make matters worse. Just let me handle it," she replied sadly, while I looked at her with pity before shaking my head sadly.

"Don't worry about me. Just go to your room I want to be left alone," she added sorrowfully.

"Why? You are yet to regain your strength. I'm not going anywhere," I replied with a heavy heart, but she calmly pushed me away from her side.

"Mary, please just go with your friend. Trust me I'm okay," she assured with red eyes. I shrugged with resignation, stood up and dragged Mariam with me as we quietly left her room.

My legs shook as I walked out from Linda's room that evening, while my heart wept as if I was the one who received the beating. Surely I was very downcast with a guilty feeling because I knew I caused the whole fight by being in her room that evening.

"Do you believe that James is a cultist?" Mariam suddenly asked as we climbed the stairs leading to our floor, instantly dragging me away from my thoughts.

"I honestly don't know dear. Life itself is a mystery," I calmly replied.

Even though I was shocked when I heard David's revelation on James' involvement in cultism, I wasn't entirely surprised because I really never liked him for once but just tolerated him because of my friend. Perhaps that was why I easily believed David's revelation even though I clearly hid my feelings from her. I didn't have the strength to take on another scene.

"I will confront him tonight," she muttered quietly.

"Good but be diplomatic when doing that," I advised. She said no other word and left for her room.

I barely had settled in my room, when Samuel's knock shook and woke me from my thoughts.

"Please dear, I'll like to be left alone," I pleaded when I opened my door. He stared at me with surprise but I looked away and avoided his gaze.

"I hope you are okay?" he asked.

"Yeah, but please, let me be for now. I'll come over to your room later," I pleaded. He stared at me for a while, shrugged and left without further questions, even though I knew his mind must be filled with questions that moment.

I couldn't help but wonder what was in Samuel's mind that evening, but my heart soon leapt when I heard someone knock on my door with David's usual way of knocking which left me stunned, speechless and indecisive as I contemplated whether to answer or not.

"What is it again?" I coldly asked David when I finally opened my door. I didn't want to answer his knock, but I was forced to when it became obvious he wasn't ready to give up knocking on my door.

In order to stop him from disturbing my neighbors whom I knew were already peeping from their respective windows to ascertain where the persistent knock disturbing them was coming from, and Samuel whom I also knew heard the noise, I had no choice than to open my door and face the devil.

"What took you so long?" he asked with a smile, expertly avoiding the question I asked him.

"What is it that you want?" I coldly asked again, while my right hand strongly held my door knob, for easy closing of my door in case he tried anything silly.

"Come on baby, why the angry look?" he asked with a composed smile. I boiled inside as I stared at him with hatred.

"How can he appear, so calm, well composed and lively after all he just did?" I wondered angrily.

"Anyway, since you don't want to talk to me, let me go ahead and say what brought me to your room," he added calmly.

"I came to apologize because of what happened this evening in Linda's room and also let you know that I did what I did just to prove to you that there is nothing going on between Linda and I anymore even though I do regret hitting her so hard," he tried to explain, but his explanation and apology only got on my nerves and infuriated me more.

"You didn't just hit the poor girl hard; you also tried to kill her. And never say that you did such a stupid thing to prove your nonsense love to me. I never sent you on such errand, so just leave me alone please," I bravely barked at him. His eyes instantly lit up in anger for a while before dying down again.

"So I lost Linda for nothing?" he asked.

"If you know what's good for you better go and apologize to her and pray she forgives you," I answered bitterly.

"Mary, please don't turn me into a wretch because you won't like it," he muttered with a dirty smile, which really shook my poor legs and frightened me.

"Are you threatening me??" I asked nervously. He just smiled and walked away, leaving me in great fear, suspense and wonder. Truly David knew how to leave a lasting impression on anyone he targeted. As he walked away, I was left in deep thought as I tried to figure out what he meant by being left a wretch.

I locked my door showered and rushed into Samuel's room, deeply shaken and scared to my bones.

"Baby, I hope you are alright?" he asked with concern.

I only came to his room that night to lose sight of David and whatever plan he had. And one thing I love about Samuel was that he never complained but was always there for me when I needed him most.

Chapter Seven

I barely had returned to my room the following morning, when Mariam knocked and entered with a very sad and tired look. She really looked that moment like a night worker who worked without rest all through the night.

She wearily fell on my bed with a sigh. I sat beside her, with both hands on my waist and stared curiously at her with surprise.

"It's over between James and I," she muttered, while I gasped in shock.

"What did you just say?" I heard myself ask.

"My relationship with James is over," she announced again, I just breathed deeply and kept quiet for a few seconds.

"How? What exactly happened?" I calmly asked.

"I confronted him last night about his ties with a cult group, he tried denying it but when I continued with my questions, he barked at me almost hitting me in the process. I gave him a condition to tell me the truth or kiss our affair goodbye, yet he ignored me till this morning when I left the room," she explained unhappily, while I smiled and held her left hand.

Even though I never supported her relationship with that boy, I knew my friend really did love him, and so I had to be cautious and neutral when advising her.

I looked at my wall clock which read 7:30AM, bit my lips and stared at my friend. I planned going to school that day but with the situation of things I knew I might skip lectures again.

"Girlfriend, are you very sure about your decision? You are already into him which is a fact you can't deny," I asked with a smile, but she kept quiet and pretended as if she didn't hear my words.

Someone knocked on my door seconds later, making me move my attention to my door. I waited extra two minutes before finally opening my door, where a nervous looking James greeted me with a forced smile.

"Is Mariam with you?" he calmly asked with a searching look. At first I was at lost on what to reply him, but when I finally made up my mind to deny ever seeing her that morning, Mariam appeared behind me and shouted at him.

"What are you doing here? Leave me alone," she barked before shutting the door on his face. Instead of leaving, he surprised us by knocking again for almost an hour, and it appeared he wasn't ready to leave my door alone until it was opened.

I was uncomfortable and a bit sad, because I already had missed lectures for that day and still trapped in my room all because I was standing by my friend.

"I think you should have a little chat with him. You never can tell what he wants to say to you," I finally whispered to Mariam when I couldn't endure his knock anymore. She tried to argue, but I gave her no chance, stood up and opened my door for James who quickly rushed to her side.

I never believed or dreamt that someone like James could ever do such a thing for a girl.

"Is that what true love really means or is he just trying to defend his pride??" was the question I kept asking myself as I left them alone in my room to fetch a bucket of water downstairs.

I ran into Linda when I finally got downstairs. I smiled politely and stopped by her side. She was well dressed up that morning, with a big pink handbag slung on her right shoulder. The events of the previous evening instantly came, racing into my mind and I glanced at her injured beauty with a heart filled with pain.

"Hi dear, are you going to school?" I asked with a look of surprise, because after what happened the previous day I never expected she could even have the strength to dress up for an outing.

"No, I'm going over to a friend's house. I'll stay there until I recover," she explained with a weak smile. I truly was touched.

"That's a nice idea dear, I'll keep praying for you," I muttered with a friendly pat on her left shoulder. She nodded with a smile and left without another word. I felt like crying that moment, but I held myself and walked to the water-pump, which unfortunately wasn't working that morning. With a deep sigh I went to the extreme of the backyard where the second water pump was situated and equally where David and his friends do stay most of the time, smoking and doing some weight-lifting exercises, making that corner of our lodge highly avoided by students. But I had no choice than to go there, since I badly needed water.

I slowly went there with a fast beating heart, and just like I feared David and two guys sat beside the water-pump discussing seriously. I muttered some greetings which they ignored before quietly fetching water from the Tap.

"I will be in your room later," I heard David mutter with a serious look as I carried the heavy bucket of water I fetched. I said nothing to him, though I managed to force out a smile, which I knew he interpreted wrongly.

I slowly returned to my room with my thoughts focused on how to end his disturbance. Nothing so far had been able to stop him and with Linda finally out of the way, I knew I was in for a bigger trouble, and it just looked like I jumped out from a burning pot only to land on the fire underneath.

"Oh Lord, please don't let this fire burn Samuel as-well," I prayed as I stepped into my room.

Perhaps it was my thought that blinded me or my fears that clouded my sight and prevented me from seeing Mariam and James engaged in a scuffle. It was too late to avert disaster as James' falling body crashed on me without warning. My head smashed on the wall, while his elbow broke my lips. My bucket instantly fell, watering my room in the process. Mariam screamed in panic.

James quickly composed himself, helped me to my feet and muttered some quick apologies. He was very embarrassed and avoided meeting my gaze.

Mariam quickly overcame her shock, rushed to my balcony, grabbed a clean piece of rag and started scrubbing my room. James joined her moments later, when he saw that I was alright. I quickly carried my books which were neatly arranged on the floor and spread them out on my balcony to dry.

Truly the whole scene came as a shock and surprise to me, but it was an accident so I blamed no one. Surprisingly, James and Mariam worked harmoniously together like newly married couples as they scrubbed my room, their quarrels forgotten as if it never happened. I smiled in appreciation as I watched them, even though I still felt a little pain on my head.

"James is really a nice guy," I finally admitted to myself, because he displayed some attributes which I never knew were in him. "Sometimes casually reading a person doesn't really tell us all we need to know, and most times we end up forming a very negative opinion about such person due to our casual observation," I reasoned with a sigh.

I quickly fried plantain which we all ate together. I almost bursted into laughter as I watched James trying so hard to make Mariam smile.

"Please help me plead to your friend, she doesn't understand how much I love her," he finally pleaded to me. I blushed and stared at Mariam without knowing what to tell her.

"Don't give me that look Mary, he should first tell me if he truly belongs to a cult group or not, if he really wants me," she fired back. I stared at James with a shrug. He instantly looked down as if he was given a very difficult condition.

"Will the truth change anything?" he asked seconds later.

"I don't know," she replied haughtily.

"Yes, I do belong to a cult group," he muttered with a deep breath.

A huge terrifying silence fell in my room as his confession registered into our heads.

For the first time, I wished he had lied.

What will become of their relationship?

"No it's a lie," Mariam screamed with a loud voice, while James humbly knelt by her side like a condemned servant.

I was very shocked and stunned with his confession, because even though he did the right thing by saying the truth, it looked that moment like he just poured water over a raging petrol fire.

I was very much at loss on what to do, and in a vegetable state I was as I watched the whole drama keenly. Mariam looked like someone who just saw a ghost with the way her eyes blazed that moment.

I don't doubt some folks who always argue that sometimes "a sweet well told lie is hundred times better than a bitter truth". The tensed up situation that morning was enough to seal my belief.

"Baby it really doesn't change who I am. Please don't let it come between us," I heard James beg. But his effort only earned him a dirty slap whose sound echoed in my room, leaving a huge lump in my throat.

"So you took me for granted all these while?" she barked like an angry wolf, while James gently rubbed his left chin where the hot slap landed. Surely that slap was so hot and terrifying. Only the force with which it was delivered, and the sound which erupted from it was enough to deafen his ear for months. Yet he still knelt humbly as if the slap was nothing but a friendly pat.

Oh what a man!

"Leave this room right now," my friend barked, pushing him backwards in a violent manner. I instantly jumped up in his defense.

"Girl you are taking this too far, chill nau," I begged with a slightly raised tone, which made her stare at me with a surprised look.

I wasn't blind not to notice that my friend was using her annoyance to abuse her boyfriend, who probably thought he was doing the right thing by calmly receiving the whole tantrum thrown at him. I knew Mariam clearly wasn't with her mind and was extremely blinded with fury, which left me with no other choice than to intervene.

"So you are now defending him, abi? How am I sure you two aren't into this together," Mariam accused with an angry scowl.

"Oh Christ," I exclaimed….

"James, please can you leave us alone," I calmly asked James who looked at me curiously.

"Don't worry you will hear from us this evening," I assured him with a faint smile. He shrugged, stood up and left without another word.

I instantly faced Mariam furiously with hands on my waist after James had left.

"What was that outburst all about? What is even wrong with you? What has gotten over you?" I asked angrily, but she just kept quiet and bit her lips.

"Please you should learn how to control your anger you are a girl. I won't involve myself in your problems again. For all I care you can go pour kerosene on him and strike a match-stick," I barked before lying down on my bed.

I was very bitter and angry over her annoying comment, which made me pour out my whole mind to her without reservation, even though I later regretted it especially when I noticed the remorse in her eyes. She truly was in a sorry state but such misguided comments are what I can never tolerate.

"I'm sorry," I heard her apologize moments later. An apology which I knew took out much effort from her.

"Sorry" is a word which really has the capability of stopping fights, quarrels, disputes and even wars, but it's also a very simple word which is very hard to say, considering our pride, because it means you accept being at fault.

"Come on nah stop vexing. You know I wasn't myself when I made that comment eeh," she pleaded and tickled me. I smiled sat up and faced her.

"It's okay, let's forget about it," I muttered with a smile, which made her hug me gratefully. Truly, Mariam really wasn't the quarrelsome type and that also made our friendship very strong as if we were sisters.

"What do you think I should do about James?" I soon heard her ask.

"It all depends on you and how you still feel about him," I replied,

"I still do love him even though I hate to admit it, and I don't know the reason I'm still feeling this way. You know how much I hate cultism and cultists," she poured out with a coloured face.

"My dear, love is a very strong feeling which can't be easily erased, moreover I just noticed he is a nice guy, so maybe it's your destiny to change and lead him towards the right path. I can only advice you to be careful and hold back a little portion of your heart," I advised.

"Don't you," she tried to argue, but I instantly placed a finger on her lips,

"Sshhh, I know you didn't sleep last night, so lie down, sleep and think it over," I advised like a nursery school teacher. She shrugged and obeyed without another word.

I smiled, lay beside her, took a novel from my travelling bag and began reading it. Soon, I found myself in fantasy land, a land of bright hopes where good dreams come true.

"I'm going back to him," My dear friend announced to me, when she finally woke up around 4pm.

"That's cool dear," I replied happily.

"But please you will follow me to his room," she begged, I shrugged and accepted.

An hour later after freshening up, we walked to James' room together and knocked calmly on his door.

He opened his door seconds later, breathed deeply with hopeful eyes when he saw us. Mariam winked at me before hugging him passionately. A very surprised James held her tightly and thanked me with his eyes.

I instantly turned and left for my room with tears of joy, satisfaction and relief in my eyes.

Chapter Eight

My heart jumped when I saw David standing beside my door. I instantly felt like turning and going back to James' room, but I couldn't. His right hand was on my door which showed he probably must have been knocking on it for long. I frowned and walked up to him.

"What do you want?" I asked coldly, he scoffed and fed his eyes on me for a while.

"Hmmm, what a question, of course I want you dear," he replied with bright eyes which got me more annoyed. Just that moment Samuel came out from his room, stood beside his door and beckoned on me to come. He probably had heard the conversation going on between David and I from his room which made him to show up that moment. But his action provoked David whose beaming eyes instantly burned furiously. He grabbed my right hand roughly and stared at me murderously.

"You are not going anywhere. He should come here and tell you whatever he wants to say," he said angrily, while I stared at him with confusion written all over my face.

Samuel saw his action as a challenge and walked up to him bravely. I felt like fainting that moment because I knew what was about to happen won't in any way be pleasant.

"Guy, abeg free my girl. I won't beg you again," Samuel warned courageously.

"Your girl, eeh? So you no longer have fear or respect in you?" David asked with a dirty smile.

"Samuel please let me handle this," I begged, but he ignored me and faced him defiantly.

David calmly freed my hand and held Samuel's shirt by the collar.

"What do you think you can do to me stinking jew?" he asked before slapping him. I panicked and instantly threw myself on Samuel who was already in the process of returning the slap. He really was no fighter or match for David who might end up calling for backup.

Instead of calming down when he saw me hold Samuel, he pulled a belt from his trouser and flung wildly without caring whether it will land on me or not.

Perhaps he did it intentionally for me to know I wasn't safe with Samuel or maybe as punishment for rejecting him.

The belt soon landed on my back with full force, sending a horrifying message of pain all across my body, yet I still held Samuel strongly and screamed for help

Luckily, neighbors rushed out from their rooms and held David strongly, even though none of them dared caution him. I managed to drag Samuel to his room, while some kind neighbors followed and assisted me in calming him down.

"Why were you fighting with that criminal?"

"Nawa for you oo."

"Do you want to bring yourself down to his level?"

"Abeg always ignore him the way we do, he is just a frustrated criminal."

They asked, advised and cautioned Samuel who kept moving his eyes to and fro like a cornered rat.

"I think you should report him to the police or school security," a neighbor advised.

"Hmmm which kind advice you dey give so? Abeg don't listen to him jare unless you are ready to fight his entire cult group," another neighbor chipped in, instantly causing a hot debate among them and it lasted till late in the evening.

"I'm sorry for dragging you into this," I apologized when we were finally alone. He bit his lips and stared at me with a blank expression.

"Mary, I failed you," he muttered sadly. My heart melted, I drew close and held him passionately.

"You made me very proud today dear," I replied sweetly. He breathed deeply before giving me a tight hug.

"Please I will like to see the spot where his belt landed on you," he begged quietly. I instantly looked away with a coloured face.

I never knew he noticed when David's belt landed on my body because it happened in a flash and I didn't mention it to him because I didn't want him to feel bad.

"Oh my God!" he exclaimed as he examined where I was hit by David's belt.

"I will report him to the police," I heard him mutter. My heart instantly leapt. I turned and held his hand.

"Please allow this matter to die, I beg, dear," I pleaded with guilt and shame in my eyes because I never knew I would stoop so low as to beg on David's behalf, even though I was restrained from reporting him to the authorities few days ago. My plea really was for Samuel's good, because cultists are always very deadly and unpredictable.

"So what do you think we should do to him?" I soon heard him ask. I swallowed hard, covered my face with my palms and rested it on my knees.

"What really should be done to that rascal?" I asked myself over and over again. A multi million question very hard to answer.

I was very busy with my thoughts that I never knew when he left me to boil hot water, or when he returned with a hot bowl of water to press the wound caused by David's belt-whip.

Days later, David saw me as I was returning from school, caught up with me at the staircase and held my right hand softly. I stopped and stared at him coldly while he returned my look with a calm smile.

"I know you are still very angry with me over what happened the other day. I'm very sorry," he apologized. I tried to snatch my hand from his grasp but he strongly held me.

"Please just take this and buy something for yourself. I really do apologize with all my heart," he muttered and offered a brown envelope to me. I stared at him speechlessly, tried again to snatch my hand but he still held it strongly.

"Just take it please," he pleaded.

"Just let me be, David," I replied with a raised tone. He stared around, before facing me once again.

"Mary what I feel for you is no ordinary love, I swear I can pull down any building just to make you mine," he added quietly.

I unhappily shook my head as I tried to calm myself down. A new plan instantly rushed into my mind.

"Okay, let's go to my room," I muttered coldly. He smiled, released my hand and together we walked to my room.

He quietly sat on my bed. I sat beside him in a well composed manner and faced him with a fake smile.

"I really do appreciate the gift, but I cannot accept it," I calmly said to him, while he silently stared at me.

"I know you truly do love me, David," I added and held his right hand which totally surprised him.

"A great love, even if it be unfortunate, should enable a man, not make him desperate and heartless. Please let's just be friends, I do believe with time I may learn to love you," I murmured gently.

"But can't you offer something much more than ordinary friendship?" He asked instantly, his anguish very real, not feigned in any way. Love, life, liberty were all at stake which I very well knew and so had to choose my words carefully.

"No, David, friendship is all I can offer for now. Here you are offering me love, and my hand does not tremble, my heart equally does not. Your words give me no pleasure, only pain; I'm conscious of nothing, only a wish to end this interview, please do understand my plight. How else can I explain that I feel no love for you at the moment," I poured out to him.

"But with time, could you learn to love me?" he eagerly asked.

"Yes, I'm very sure I will. Please don't think I speak out of pride or to hurt you," I lied sweetly. All I wanted that moment was my freedom which I prayed our little discussion would grant me.

I saw a sudden shadow of despair come into his eyes. I swallowed hard and muttered quick silent prayers to my creator.

"You have unmanned me, but I think you are right, I can't force out love from you, let's be friends like you said," he muttered while his cheeks flushed with embarrassment.

I heaved a sigh of relief, my eyes instantly lit up with joy. I felt like hugging him in appreciation, but I held myself.

"Thanks a lot for understanding my plight," I murmured with delight.

He stood for some moments in silence; a dim perception of his own unworthiness came over him, with a smile, he tapped my left shoulder and left my room quietly.

"Is this the end?" I asked myself happily.

David never did disturb me again. He just kept his distance and avoided me like a snake which I very much loved. It really was very surprising to Samuel who couldn't believe that David easily swallowed his pride and gave me up without any harm.

Chapter Nine

Time flies so fast when we have our dreams up and running. I was soon in the second semester of my third year while Samuel in his final semester as a student.

Our relationship blossomed and matured into something so solid and sweet, despite the fact that we abstained from sex. It just looked as if I was created for him. His family accepted and treated me as if I was their daughter. They really couldn't wait for us to finish school and get married.

I transformed Samuel from a quiet, cool headed introvert into an artistic, charming, noble young man whose greatest hobby was to love me. The clothes in my wardrobe, the jewelleries, flowers, cards, teddy bears I was lavished with and even my fat bank account all testified to his benevolence. He so totally spoilt me, that I hardly ever touched the monthly allowance my parents did gave me. My ego and pride were so high. I was envied by many.

"Oh what else could I have asked my creator for?"

Love surely works wonders.

But sometimes no matter how hard we struggle to shape our future, challenges do come to test our courage and zeal, always appearing when least expected, and only a little misdeed that moment could rewrite everything.

Some folks do say that 'whatever will be, will surely be no matter how hard we plan,' and some holy books do say 'our destiny already has been written by our creator before birth.' Whatever the case, life is so full of mysteries.

The future I so much struggled to build with Samuel was completely jeopardized weeks into my 300 level second semester. I never knew my fate could take neither such a dramatic twist nor my past showing up to haunt me. Not only did it return to haunt me, it equally came to steal my soul, pride, heart and all I labored for, without even a mask to hide its face.

My past came pertinaciously for me when I least expected, and I truly can't explain how lost or petrified I was when it came knocking on my door.

The shock, pain and anger I felt when I answered my door and saw Emmanuel, my ex-boyfriend, smiling nervously with hands clasped behind him, was so immense that I couldn't breathe for a while. The look of relief in his eyes when they rested on me really was undeniable. For some seconds I stared at him speechlessly, lost in thought and clueless on what to do.

He truly wasn't looking bad, though a bit darker than when I last saw him. He wore a white shirt, black tie, trouser and shoes. His features perfectly constructed and matured.

How fast I noticed.

"Nooooo, go away!" I cried as I shut my door on his face, dived to my bed and covered my head with my pillow.

"How did he find me?" I wondered miserably.

I left my old lodge and changed my phone number all because of him. Seeing him that afternoon instantly brought up old memories, drawing out tears from my eyes. I was highly demoralized.

"Mary, please open your door, I just came to talk with you," he knocked and begged. I simply ignored him and refused to open my door.

He finally left after an hour of constant knocking. I heaved a sigh of relief and made the sign of the cross.

"Lord, please be my strength," I prayed, because I needed no one to tell me that he would return. However, I failed to mention Emmanuel's visit to Samuel when we were together later in the evening without knowing the reason. Perhaps it was because I didn't want to involve him in my problems anymore. A lame excuse I consoled my guilt with.

"Is everything alright?" Samuel asked curiously as soon as he noticed my absent-mindedness

"I'm having a slight headache," I muttered calmly.

"I have some Paracetamol in my room, let me get it for you," he sweetly said as he got up.

"No don't worry, all I need is just a good night sleep," I said and flashed him a smile. He shrugged and rubbed my back.

"Good night dear, let me leave you alone," he muttered and left for his room.

***

"Some lecturers are truly very annoying with the manner they behave sometimes," I murmured furiously as I left our lecture hall after writing a hot impromptu test which I only managed to answer three out of six questions. I was very annoyed and swore to anyone who blocked my path as I left the hall as if something was pursuing me.

A strong hand grabbed me without warning. I instantly turned to lash out on whoever it might be. But I was stunned when my eyes fell on Emmanuel, smiling nervously in his usual way. I felt like slapping him but the crowd around us was much.

"Calm down my dear. Some things are not always as they seem," he said calmly. "I have a story to tell. After listening to it you can then pour out your mind," he added.

"I'm in no mood to listen to your story. I don't care anymore. Moreover it's too late," I replied haughtily. I could have snatched my hand and ran away that moment, but I didn't, instead I stood and stared at him while I silently deliberated whether to listen to his story or not. Curiosity got a better part of me, perhaps.

"Don't say anything dear, until you listen to my story. It won't take much of your time. You can go your way after listening to it. I only came to fulfill something I promised myself," he urged with a smile. I breathed deeply, shrugged with a shoulder and followed him to a quiet, expensive cafe at the other end of the school.

I knew it was undignifying to allow my curiosity get hold of me, but I just couldn't help it.

"Am I under a spell or what?" I asked myself as we sat down in the cafe, moments later.

"Please, God, don't allow Samuel see me here," I silently prayed with guilt.

"Please be quick with the story," I said with a drawn face, while he simply just smiled, supported his jaw with his right hand and stared at me like someone with a whole lot of time in his hands.

"You really have grown into a beautiful woman, sexier and more attractive than I expected," he said with a smile. I frowned and sighed.

"Your plan didn't work. You thought I will dry up like a dead leaf when you abandoned me, abi? Mtcheeew" I poured and hissed. He instantly looked away with remorse in his eyes, but I felt no pity for him. His comment really ignited my anger, even though it was meant to flatter me.

"Abeg do fast and tell me the story, I have other things to do," I urged coldly.

"Your comments are just like a whip, flogging the living hell out of me," he murmured in order to draw out pity. I scoffed, shook my head and stared at him coldly.

Thunder fire you there. I just wish my comments could do much more than flogging your wretched body," I cursed bitterly.

"My God! Mary you have changed considerably. You now curse and throw insults without fear," he exclaimed with surprise.

"Change is a constant thing in life oga, and as long as I'm alive, I will keep on changing. By the way I see you have no story to tell so this conversation is over and never happened," I barked and stood up rudely. He instantly tried to grab my left hand, but was unsuccessful.

"Please don't ever come to my lodge again unless you need a hot bath," I threatened and walked away, while he speechlessly stared at me with a coloured face.

"God, please forgive me. I never intended to curse and insult him this way, but you know he caused everything," I prayed with remorse as I left the cafe.

I soon felt a strong hand grab me from behind outside the cafe, I instantly turned and stared at Emmanuel murderously,

"Please can I have your phone number," he begged.

"Go to hell," I cursed, turned and made to leave. He instantly blocked my path and stared at me with prayers in his eyes.

"Don't do this, Mary, please. I have waited so long for this moment. If you refuse me your phone number, I will have no choice than to follow you to your lodge and kill myself with your hot water. I can't just continue living this way, not after seeing you after a long wait," he begged seriously.

I looked up and down with confusion and frustration quickly eating me up like hunger. I equally battled with my mind as I thought of the strategy I could use in discharging him.

I slowly held my pride, and controlled my angry spirit.

"I need to sleep over this issue. I can't just give you my new phone number easily. Moreover, you just appeared from the clouds after disappearing from my life for a long time. I will be in school tomorrow, perhaps you will get my number if we meet then, but please on no account should you visit my lodge. That's all I can say for now and I think it's fair considering all you did to me," I said calmly. He shrugged unhappily and nodded with a faint smile.

"That's fine by me," he accepted without another argument. I rolled my eyes and walked away without another word.

"How do I resist this idiot of a boy?" I wondered.

"I surely need Mariam's advice before I do something nasty. Two heads, they say, are better than one," I concluded with a calm smile as I trekked back to my lodge, very glad I was finally free from his disturbance, at least for that day.

***

"Emmanuel is back," I whispered into my friend's ear, later that day, as if I was scared of calling out Emmanuel's name. She glanced at me with surprise.

"Emmanuel! Which Emmanuel?" she curiously asked.

"My ex na, have you forgotten him?" I replied. She instantly gasped and held my left palm tightly.

"You mean you saw him?" she asked,

"He was in my room yesterday and even blocked me in school today," I explained.

"So what does he want? How did he even find you?" she asked with concern.

"Girl, I really can't say how he found me. I even thought you were the person who helped him," I answered quietly. She gave me an askance look, smiled and tapped my left shoulder.

"Nawa for you, why you go think that kind thing? I'm very much surprised as you are. So what did he say and what does he want?" she asked.

"Usual stuff, he wants my phone number, he has a story to tell, he can't continue living this way," I replied and mimicked Emmanuel's voice. She laughed and clapped her hands.

"Abegi don't mind him. Better be careful from now onwards. You know how guys, especially first boyfriends can be very cunning and crafty like con-artists. Moreover he knows you too well, so please don't even give him any chance to open his mouth," she advised.

"But how can I do that? He threatened to kill himself if I don't give him attention," I murmured.

"Then let him kill himself. Supposing you died of heartbreak when he left you, would he be talking all these nonsense." she replied quite upset, while I breathed deeply and shrugged.

"So have you told your guy?" she asked.

"No," I murmured and shook my head.

"Please don't hide this issue from him. It will be easier for you to discharge him with Samuel backing you up. I'm talking from experience," she advised like a sister. And that was a good advice from Mariam which I turned down. A great mistakes we ladies make when our Ex later shows up from nowhere.

"I really don't like involving that poor boy in my problems," I murmured,

"I don't think you have any other choice, my dear," she concluded and stared at me with pity. I looked away and shrugged.

***

At about 9PM that evening, I was in Samuel's room. I lay on his chest, while he gently played with my hair, a gesture I always enjoyed but that evening, I really was very restless.

Mariam's advice kept reoccurring in my head, urging me to open up and reveal all I was hiding but I couldn't get myself to do her bidding which was the most appropriate thing to do.

A force I could neither define nor figure out sealed my lips and locked them firmly like a padlock. Perhaps it was fear which hindered me or maybe it was my stupidity which played such a dirty trick on me. My conscience urged me but my strength failed me, while my mouth refused to oblige. The kind of force which held me that moment seemed similar to that which often stops us girls from exposing our boyfriend's pals who make passes at us. Only girls will surely understand the state I was in. Deep down I felt very guilty.

"I will talk to Emmanuel tomorrow, if he still insists, then I will have no choice than to tell Samuel," I promised myself.

A promise which left a sour feeling in my mind, but unknown to me Mariam had her own plans which soon reshaped and turned everything upside down for me.

Chapter Ten

Dawn arrived quicker than I expected. I tossed uneasily on Samuel's bed.

"How do I face Emmanuel today?" I wondered and closed my eyes.

"God help me," I prayed and breathed deeply. My strength failed me.

I stayed away from lectures that day, and stayed indoors with Samuel, who really had no problem with sacrificing his lectures because of me. We had a wonderful time playing and joking. He never went beyond his boundary, a thing I liked most about him. Deep within me I still felt very uneasy.

I kept thinking about Emmanuel and his next line of action since I failed to show up in school. My heart leapt each time I heard someone knocking on a neighbor's door, fearing it was him knocking on my door.

"Are you okay, babe? You look very anxious and uneasy," Samuel asked numerous times. But instead of telling him my plight I preferred to keep it firmly sealed in my heart.

***

"I can't believe you still haven't told him about Emmanuel, upon everything I said to you yesterday. Seriously you are no longer behaving like the Mary I know, are you under a spell or you still harbor some form of affection for that boy?" Mariam asked suspiciously, when she came into my room later in the evening, after returning from school.

"You won't understand," I murmured and bit my lips.

"Yes I can't understand your behavior anymore. You even skipped lectures because of that boy," she replied and shook her head.

"I know what I'm doing, okay. You are just misunderstanding my actions dear," I murmured. She shrugged and changed the topic, while I instantly felt relieved. I really had no strength to argue with her.

However when Samuel confronted me about Emmanuel later in the night, I knew my best friend had snitched on me. I felt very terrible, weak and lost, but what pained me the most was Samuel's words. They injured me immensely.

"I never knew you could keep such information away from me. I never believed I will ever hear such news from someone else. Why, Mary? Why?" he asked after repeating all Mariam told him.

I swallowed hard and looked away, with an injured pride, totally ashamed of myself.

"I can't even imagine you stayed away from school just because of him," he muttered.

"Baby I kept it away from you because I didn't want to involve you. I knew how upset you would be if I told you such news," I explained truthfully, but for the first time he choose not to believe me. He stared at me for a while before looking down.

"I honestly don't know what to believe. How am I even sure you haven't been meeting him secretly? Perhaps it was your friend's conscience that made her open up to me even though I suspect she tuned down the whole thing," he accused bitterly. I gasped in shock, grabbed his right hand strongly, forcing him to bring his eyes back on me.

For the first time, Samuel doubted and suspected me. He had also never spoken silly words to me before. But that moment, it appeared as if I lost all his trust. The most painful part of it all was that he accused me unjustly and kept staring at me as though I were a half penny whore.

"My God, why would Mariam do this to me?" I wondered with a weeping heart, totally lost, dejected and heartbroken.

"Good night," Samuel muttered, snatched his hand from my grasp, and turned his back on me.

"Where are you going?" I asked stupidly,

"To my room of course," he replied coldly.

"Spend the night here with me dear?" I begged,

"I don't think it's necessary. You never wanted me to get involved so it is better I stay away so that you can clean up your problems alone just like you wanted. You can notify me when you are done," he said and left my room.

"Dear, your behavior is punishing me. Don't leave me here alone, please," I begged as he left.

I never knew Samuel could ever get so annoyed with me. It just looked like my life was crashing in a terrifying manner.

I spent that night tossing on my bed and crying. I woke up the next day emotionally weak, perturbed and uneasy.

Mariam showed up in my room by 7:55AM, I felt like murdering her, but had to control myself because I didn't want to create a scene with someone so vulgar.

"Why the drawn face huh?" she asked and sat beside me with concern. I sighed and looked the other way.

"Snitch," I hissed quietly,

"Hmmm okay, now I understand the monkey face you are showing me. Of course I told Samuel because you have no reason for hiding Emmanuel's disturbance from him. You won't understand what I did for you. You will definitely thank me later," she patted my back and laughed.

"This is no laughing matter. Your big mouth just cost me my relationship," I cried.

"Abegi make I hear word jare," she replied and fell back on my bed.

"I'm very serious. Samuel almost pounced on me yesterday," I complained bitterly. To my surprise, my dear friend laughed out loud.

"Anyway I don't blame you. I caused everything by revealing my problems to you," I added sadly. She sat up and stared at me seriously.

"Babe, don't talk like that. Samuel loves you very much. He just reacted as he should. Relax he will come back to make peace," she assured.

"What if he doesn't?" I asked,

"Then you go yourself and beg him. You have legs, don't you?" she replied and winked at me, "anyway I don't think Samuel can last a day without you" she concluded while I shrugged.

We argued and debated about Emmanuel, Samuel and how to settle my problems throughout that morning till 11:30AM when we heard a steady knock on my door interrupting us.

Mariam quickly answered my door and froze when she saw who was knocking. She slowly walked backwards like someone possessed by an evil power. My face instantly coloured. I gasped and swallowed hard when I saw Emmanuel confidently walk into my room with a steady smile. But before I could recover from the shock, Mariam quickly regained herself and pushed him ferociously with an energy I never had seen in her.

Her push took him by surprise, and sent him staggering backwards towards the open door. Mariam pushed again and again until he was out of my room without much resistance. She quickly locked my door with great speed and rested her body against it as she gasped for breath.

I really was totally stunned, and surprised at the great stunt she pulled. I stared at her gratefully for some minutes and breathed deeply.

"God, please give me the type of mind, strength and courage Mariam has," I prayed.

"That guy is something else. Imagine the arrogance, the smile and the way he carried himself, God," Mariam cried and fell on my bed.

"Do you think your action will stop him?" I asked with a smile.

"Of course not, what I did was just a temporary measure. Stopping him permanently is in your hands, just like you did to David," she replied.

"But I think you should first apologize and sort out your differences with Samuel before having anything to do with that rascal, or else you will be compounding issues and further complicating them," she lectured, "imagine allowing him into your room and Samuel shows up in the process," she added. A shiver ran through me as I imagined it all.

"You are right dear, I will settle with Samuel this evening," I assured her.

Emmanuel knocked on my door for hours and left when he realized nothing would make us open the door for him. Mariam later left for her own room. I bathed, wore a lovely gown and some nice perfume all over my body and went over to Samuel's room.

He allowed me into his room without saying anything. I smiled, lay on his bed and stared at him. He sat on his rug and backed me, focusing his eyes on the TV screen, even though it was obvious his mind was somewhere else.

"I'm sorry," I quietly apologized and touched his right shoulder. He kept quiet and ignored me.

"You know me better dear, and you know the last thing I will ever do is to cheat on you, not with my ex, not with anyone," I prayed.

"I don't know you anymore," he muttered coldly. I breathed deeply, climbed down from the bed and sat beside him on the floor.

"Dear, look into my eyes and tell me you don't know me anymore. I won't disturb you again if you look into my eyes and say it," I dared him calmly. He looked into my eyes momentarily before looking away. I smiled and heaved a sigh of relief.

"I still have much control over him," I acknowledged.

I gently pecked him, cutting off his tirade. For a brief instant he resisted, then sighed.

"It wounds me when you act like this," I murmured,

"Isn't there something you need to tell me?" he asked curiously. I looked away and played the feminine stunt. Tears fell from my eyes and I began to cry.

He instantly clasped me to his chest

"Ssh," he soothed. "It's over. Everything is alright."

I smiled in my mind, searched his face as I probed for equivocation but encountered none, making me ultimately accept his pledge to be genuine.

"Problem solved," I breathed deeply and murmured to myself. My dearest Samuel is the most gullible guy I have ever met. Maybe it was so because he loved me with all his heart.

"Why are you smiling?" I soon heard him ask. But I didn't reply because I was busy planning my next line of action, which was stopping Emmanuel from disturbing me. I felt uneasy thinking about it as if I knew my downfall was approaching.

"Please, my love, don't ever mistrust me again," I whispered pleadingly into his ear. He swiftly turned and stared into my eyes with the cutest smile ever.

"It won't happen again dear," he promised and pecked me. I smiled gratefully, played with his left ear for a while before playfully pinching his jaw.

"I have another request to make my love," I carefully murmured. He held my left hand and nodded for me to continue.

"Please allow me to handle Emmanuel the way I deem fit," I begged humbly. His expression instantly changed, and he breathed deeply like someone in pain, as he scanned my face with his eyes like a detective.

"Baby I don't think it's wise," he tried to argue. I instantly placed a finger on his lips, deliberately stopping him from finishing his objection.

"Please baby," I begged with my feminine charms. He looked away for some seconds, shrugged and faced me again.

"Alright, if that will make you happy and equally get him to leave you then there is no reason to object," he accepted with a dry smile, while my eyes instantly beamed with joy. I hugged him happily, every pore in my body smiled with excitement.

"Thanks my love. You are the best; very understanding and considerate," I commended happily, before resting on his body like a little child.

He just held me and smiled like someone who displeased himself for the sake of peace.

"Do you think you can handle Emmanuel on your own," Mariam asked with concern the following morning, after listening to the narration I gave her on how I secured Samuel's love and trust again.

"Yeah, I can. Don't you trust me anymore?" I answered and stared at her suspiciously. Seriously her behavior and loyalty seemed to change, since she learnt of Emmanuel's return.

"I do trust you dear," she flashed a quick smile, shrugged and expertly changed the topic.

***

I was about taking my usual Sunday siesta when I heard gentle knocks on my door. I lazily got up from my bed,

86

opened my door and gasped in surprise when my eyes fell on Emmanuel smiling nervously. I felt weak on my knees, while my heart skipped a bit. I didn't know why I always felt uneasy each time I met his gaze. "Perhaps I really haven't gotten over him the way I thought," I wondered as I stared coldly at him.

"Mary, all I need is just two minutes of your time. Please don't shut your door on me. Just grant me audience," he begged softly. I breathed deeply and allowed him into my room, very determined to end his chapter and disturbance that afternoon.

"Thanks for letting me into your room," Emmanuel murmured with a smile as he settled down on a small plastic chair.

"I know what I came to say may be a bit difficult and probably weird to you, but I truly came with every bit of sincerity and honesty a guy could ever muster. Before I begin please let's keep all our differences and things of the past aside and think only about the future," he fluently poured out. I scoffed, held my jaw and nodded for him to continue.

"I know I did a very terrible, unforgivable deed by abandoning you. I truly do apologize for that and I know if you will ever bear to hear my side of the story, you really will understand why it happened. Anyway let me go straight to why I came here," he added nervously like a new bank executive who was making his first presentation. My heart pounded furiously as I listened to him.

"Baby, I came to finish the dream we started together years ago. Remember the plans, hopes and dreams we shared. The drawings and promises we made to each other as we mapped our life years ago. I have returned with the noble intention of finishing it. Let's forget the past and forge ahead, please. I now work with Fidelity bank, just like I told you I will when I graduate. Please don't let personal feelings and anger cloud your judgment. My parents are waiting for you, my heart very eager to unite with yours and my soul could only be at rest with you by my side. Mary dear, let's finish this dream together," he pleaded passionately.

"Stop!" I snapped, cutting off his speech midway. I truly couldn't believe his words were having terrible effects on me. I really was hypnotized.

"What's wrong with me, why am I even listening to all this thrash," I wondered, terribly alarmed at the apparent change in me. I instantly trembled when I felt his touch as he expertly reached out, held my fingers and knelt by my side, noticing how shaken I was.

"I see confusion in your eyes. But please think this through. Remember how we started and remember that I do know you very well. I went to conquer the world, now I'm back with the spoils which I lay at your feet. Please listen to the silent whispers in your heart," he persuaded like a devil, confusing me more.

I was lost, confused and alarmed. My heart yearned for one thing while my body demanded for another. Sure he really was my first love, but aren't old memories supposed to fade with time?

"I'll be back for your reply Mary," he whispered and kissed me before I could even breathe twice or say anything. His kiss so bitter but very strong shook my hormones so terribly that I gasped for air.

Before I could get myself to look up at him, he was gone.

"Lord, help me," I prayed. I knew I finally had gotten a very terrible secret to hide from everyone.

"Not even Mariam will hear of this," I concluded to myself. "How shameful it will be if she finds out," I reasoned as I wondered how to overcome the terrible effect Emmanuel's disturbance was having on me.

What should I have done??

Chapter Eleven

I couldn't sleep that Sunday, neither the next day nor the day after, as my body, soul and spirit revolted. They clashed and fought each other for supremacy over the control of my heart. I was terribly lost, dejected and confused. I really couldn't believe I was thinking over Emmanuel's request or considering seeing him again.

"Am I still in love with him? Why am I having all these confusions in my head? What of Samuel?? Am I not supposed to think only of Samuel? Am I mentally sick or what?" I kept asking myself as I searched my mind for hidden answers.

"Am I even in love with Samuel? Am I just using the poor boy to satisfy my lonely self? God, I'm finished," I do end up crying with guilt, disbelief and remorse.

I had no one to share my problems with, and Mariam who could have helped, really proved to be on Samuel's side, so I feared she might report everything to him if I opened up to her.

The week slowly crept by without Emmanuel neither showing up nor disturbing me. I tried my best to make good use of my time, concentrating on my studies and returning Samuel's love. It really helped me get back some confidence, but at night it was a terrible story. Emmanuel's image kept appearing in my head.

As a girl I carried my secrets without revealing anything to anyone. If Samuel noticed the change in me, he neither showed it nor asked any probing questions. I equally avoided Mariam to the extent I only saw her only thrice that week.

***

I was on my way to my hair dresser's salon when I ran into Emmanuel at the hostel gate.

"Why are you here?" I asked coldly. He just smiled and stared at me all over.

"I came to see you my dear, good morning," he murmured. I sighed, pushed him out of my way and walked towards my destination. He instantly ran and held my right hand strongly.

"Where are you going? I can drop you," he offered and pointed to an ash -coloured Toyota Corolla S.

"You wan show me say you don buy old model car abi?" I scoffed, gave him an askance look and tried to continue with my journey, but he still held me strongly and stared into my eyes pleadingly.

"Please it won't do you any harm. Moreover we can discuss as I drive you to wherever you are going," he pleaded. I breathed deeply, looked around, saw no familiar face within the premises, and nodded.

"Alright, but I will never enter your car ever again," I muttered.

"No problems, thanks dear," he accepted happily, rushed to his car, opened the passenger's door and helped me in. He switched on his car engine, backed out the car and stared at me searchingly.

"You can drive to Dora's Salon, I want to re-touch my hair," I commanded. He smiled, floored the accelerator and drove towards Dora's Salon.

"I never knew you still patronize her. I thought you always complained that she cuts your hair each time she touches it?" he asked. I looked away and smiled to myself.

"So he still remembers how I complained about Dora during the days we were together, years ago," I reasoned with disbelief.

We soon arrived at the hair dressing Salon. He parked his car on a good spot, killed the engine and stared at me.

"I will wait for you," he murmured.

"No don't bother, thanks," I replied a bit coldly.

"I insist dear," he strongly added. I breathed deeply, shrugged and got out from his car.

"Why do I always end up playing this dirty game with him? How will all these end?" I wondered as I walked into the salon.

He sat in his car and waited for me, while I sat in the salon and kept praying to Mother Mary to help, guide and protect me from the dangerous path I was threading.

A woman's life is very complicated and uncertain, but male folks never seem to understand or notice.

"Emmanuel we can never be together again. All I can offer you this moment is only friendship. How many times do you want me to repeat this? Please stop wasting your time with me and search for another," I implored him as we headed back to my lodge after I was done fixing my hair.

He frowned slightly, stared at me for a while and drove on silently.

Thinking over everything as I fixed my hair, I came to the conclusion that perhaps I wasn't destined to be with him. I didn't see any good reason why he even abandoned me in the first place. Yet I also couldn't deny that I wasn't feeling something for him, even though it wasn't strong enough to make me risk my relationship with Samuel.

Emmanuel drove on silently until we got to my lodge. He killed the car engine and stared at me pointedly.

"At least can I have your phone number please," he beseeched.

"No, Emmanuel, I can't. I do need to forget everything about you and so do you," I confessed. He swallowed hard, drew a bit closer and held my left hand softly.

"Why are you resisting me so strongly?" he asked quietly.

"You are not giving me fair hearing. Please allow me to explain why I kept away from you," he begged.

"No explanation can justify what you did. Please I beg of you, stop disturbing me," I pleaded, snatched my hand from his grasp and ran out of his car. He quickly followed me, but unluckily for me, I ran into Samuel who was standing beside the hostel gate with an empty plastic container in his hand.

I panicked and gasped, while Emmanuel equally stopped, stared at us for a while, turned back, entered his car and drove off as if he understood.

Samuel silently stared at me with surprise. I really was at lost on what to say or how to explain myself, because he clearly saw both of us even before we did saw him, and I knew there was no way he wouldn't put the whole scene together.

I quickly ran to my room without saying anything to him, expecting him to run after me, but he didn't, instead went ahead with his own business.

I rushed and prepared beans for lunch as I waited for him to show up, perhaps to demand for an explanation. But he didn't which further surprised and alarmed me.

With a fast beating heart, I dutifully carried two plates of beans to Samuel's room.

Since he failed to show up and have his lunch in mine, I had no choice than to take the food to his room.

He allowed me into his room with a sneer on his face, while I smiled nervously as I dropped the two plates on the rug.

"Can you explain the scene I just witnessed hours ago?" he instantly asked coldly. I swallowed hard and stared at him, clueless on how to explain the scene Emmanuel and I created. I remorsefully looked down and said nothing.

Surprisingly, he advanced and pushed me violently. I fell and somersaulted on his bed, while his fist closed in on me before I could even recover from the shock his violent push gave me. I held my breath and closed my eyes.

Samuel wasn't a violent person. I guess it was entirely my fault. Yet I felt very bitter and blamed him for concluding without proper investigation.

I closed my eyes as I nervously waited for his fist to land on me. But after waiting for some seconds, I opened my eyes and saw him staring at me with hatred and rage.

I instantly turned and attempted to run back to my room. He grabbed my hand and violently tossed me back on his bed.

"What has come over you? Get hold of yourself. Thing are not exactly as they seem," I cried as I struggled with him, trying to defend myself. He just scoffed, shook his head and bit his lips.

"I know what I saw, Mary. Or were my eyes deceiving when I saw you alight from that guy's car? Was I dreaming? Please, you can tell me," he shouted angrily.

"I have been a fool to believe your cock and bull story about ending things with him your own way. I guess you were doing it perfectly this afternoon. Unless you want to tell me the guy I saw is not your ex.

"Let me be. I see you haven't learnt to trust me after all," I shouted back, sat up and dared him.

"Trust is a silly word you girls use to deceive us. Mary I don't trust you anymore," he said coldly and bluntly. I felt insulted, dirty and wounded. I never knew a day would come when Samuel will talk back at me, let alone insult and humiliate me in such manner.

"What did you just say?" I asked angrily.

"Your recent behaviors aren't in anyway decent. I don't trust you my dear, read my lips," he shouted disrespectfully. I drew forward, slapped him and jumped out of his bed.

"Since you no longer trust me, better keep away from me," I barked angrily.

"I guess you have gotten the opportunity you are waiting for huh? You are now free to run into his arms," he taunted. I stared at him with tears in my eyes.

"I have my pride and dignity; I will never be insulted or humiliated by anyone not even you. Don't come back begging," I threatened and left his room.

I hated myself as I cried and ran to my room that moment, but it was the only thing I could do.

"How do I redeem myself? Why is Samuel behaving this way? How do I atone for my sins? Is it my fault that I still feel something for Emmanuel? Didn't I do the right thing by refusing his advances? Why am I being punished this way? God, why?" I cried.

***

Mariam walked into my room with a calm smile on her face. I wasn't happy seeing her that evening but I couldn't deny her access into my room because she was like a sister to me even though I felt she no longer was watching my back.

"I'm just coming from Samuel's room," she muttered as she sat on my bed. I carried my teddy bear, played with it and ignored her statement.

"I don't understand you anymore. You are very obnoxious these days," she added. I scoffed and rolled my eyes.

"Oh please," I retorted, while she stared at me and shook her head.

"I can't believe you are allowing Emmanuel to ruin the sweet relationship you enjoy with Samuel. Think my dear, think!" She cautioned as if she were my mother. I dropped my teddy bear and looked up at her seriously.

"Did Samuel tell you how he humiliated and almost hit me hours ago simply because he saw Emmanuel arguing with me? Would I be arguing with Emmanuel if I was giving him the green light? Abeg leave me jor, in fact I'm tired of this relationship. I want to be left alone," I poured out bitterly, while she listened to my outburst attentively with both hands on her jaw. Her face coloured with disbelief and surprise.

"I can't believe all I'm hearing. Mary, I really do think you are under a strong influence. Come on get a hold of yourself and put yourself in his shoes, wouldn't you have assumed the worst?" she asked as she drew near and held my left hand.

"Seriously dear I don't want to talk about this anymore. I want to forget about everything. Only God knows my destiny. Nothing I do can change it," I remarked seriously with pain in my heart. She shrugged and stood up in resignation.

"Good night dear friend, let me go and sleep," she murmured and left silently.

***

I sang God's praises as I prepared for 8am Sunday mass. I woke up that morning very refreshed, bright, and happy and in high spirit without actually knowing the reason.

I soon heard gentle knocks on my door as I arranged my hair. I opened my door and held my breath when I saw Samuel standing on my door-way and staring hopefully at me. I wasn't expecting him but I however wasn't surprised to see him. I knew he'd come to beg sooner or later.

I forced out a smile and made way for him to enter my room.

"Happy Sunday," I politely greeted.

"There isn't anything happy about this Sunday. Anyway I came to apologize for what happened yesterday, please forgive me," he atoned without looking at me, as if he was ashamed of what he was doing, which made me ignore him and continue with 'my church preparation'.

"Baby, please let's not allow that guy or anything to come between us. I know I overreacted yesterday and I do apologize for it," he added solemnly.

I turned, faced him, drew closer and held his hands,

"You said many hurtful things yesterday which got me thinking about our relationship. Anyway, I only have one question," I said as I searched his face curiously.

"What is it my love?" he asked quietly. I breathed deeply and continued

"I know you hardly lie to me because I haven't given you any reason to do such. Now look me in the eyes and tell me you do trust me," I prayed. But my request as simple as it was really drew out a little frown from his face. He instantly looked down and murmured something inaudible.

"Speak up dear and please look at me," I implored hopefully.

"Baby, I can't lie over such trifle request. Please let's settle our differences first. We can talk about this subject later," he answered while my face instantly fell.

"There is no relationship without love, no love without trust. I can't continue with this until you start to trust me again. I suggest you go back and build your trust," I requested with a little confidence and air.

"What!" he exclaimed loudly in disbelief and total shock. The fire in his eyes sparkled like a burning dry bush. I instantly backed away in order not to get burnt by his fury.

"I'm off to church," I said quietly as I backed away from him. He quickly held me strongly, hit his head twice with his left hand and bit his lips as he struggled with himself.

"You brought happiness into my life, now you are taking it away," he accused.

"Is that what lovers do to each other? Why are you doing this to me? Why are you behaving like a fusspot? Do you now doubt my love? Please don't turn me into a bitter person," he prayed sorrowfully.

I instantly felt guilty, terrible and remorseful. I snatched my hand from his grasp and sat on my bed, covering my face with my palms.

"You know sometimes our faith is tested with tempting issues. Please don't let our relationship crumble over this little problem. I could have walked away, cried my heart out and forgotten about you but I didn't. I easily could have waited for you to apologize, but instead I buried my pride and did the opposite. My dear what more prove do you seek concerning my love?" he poured out solemnly while my heart and eyes melted.

He knelt by my side and slowly placed his head on mine, breathing heavily as he waited for me to say something.

"Alright I have heard you. Let's continue like we used to. We both had a terrible dream yesterday that's all, let's forget about it," I said and held him tightly.

He said nothing, his happiness overwhelming him. He was a boy so much in love with me, with a kind of passion which could make any guy stupid.

Anyway, I was very glad to still have him back.

Days passed by without Emmanuel neither showing up nor disturbing my life. I knew perhaps he kept away because he had a very demanding Job.

Samuel and I used the opportunity to work on our relationship. He was always by my side as if he was my shadow. I felt he still was very suspicious and doubtful about my loyalty, but I pretended not to notice. But what happened on Monday, a week later was something I won't forget in a hurry. It was the day my past and present met and fought for supremacy. A day Samuel and Emmanuel confronted each other in my room.

The earth shook, my head ached and my heart bled.

Oh what a terrible day it was!

Chapter Twelve

"A young man came here yesterday with his Mum asking for your hand in marriage. He looked very serious and asked some prying questions like our culture demands," Mum said to me after evening meal.

"A young man?" I asked with surprise.

"Yeah, he called himself Emmanuel, a very good friend of yours," Mum added. I rolled my eyes and shook my head.

"So what did you and Dad say to him?" I asked inquisitively.

"We answered some of his questions and promised to get back to him after hearing your opinion. He then left his phone number and promised to visit within two weeks. He behaved nicely, but dear every decision is yours to make, moreover we aren't in a hurry to get you married. By the way, do you actually know the young man?" Mum explained and asked with a sweet smile.

"Yeah, I do know him, but I still have more years ahead before thinking of marriage," I replied hotly.

"Calm down dear. Like I earlier said, we your parents aren't desperate to get you married. Your Dad will call and notify him," she assured me. I smiled happily.

"Thanks Mum," I murmured and hugged her. However, I was no fool not to notice that she really liked him. The way her eyes beamed as she described him, displayed her mind like a chalkboard.

"Don't worry, I know you will like Samuel even more," I assured her in my mind.

I travelled back to school on Sunday with Emmanuel's issue weighing heavily on my mind. Emmanuel really came back fully prepared for me. His actions showed it all. But I had an obligation towards Samuel which I wasn't ready to betray even though I wasn't feeling strongly for him the way I used to.

Just like my Mum promised, Dad called and informed Emmanuel of my decision earlier that Sunday before I left the house, but the smile on his face after the phone call weakened me.

"The young man said he is willing to wait forever. Can you imagine?" Dad announced with a shrug, making my heart skip a beat.

I however, told Samuel everything that happened at home without mincing words when we were together later in the evening. He just kept quiet for a while, shook his head sadly and bit his lips.

"That sneaky fool," he cursed. I rolled my eyes, held his left hand and smiled at him reassuringly.

"Don't let it bother you dear, I'm already handling the situation," I said sweetly, but he simply scoffed, made to say something, held himself and breathed deeply as he stared at me.

"Can I have his phone number? And please don't say No," he requested a bit coldly. I shrugged, took his phone and entered Emmanuel's phone number in it.

"I don't know if he still uses it. It's the phone number he used as a student," I explained.

With a dry smile he took his phone, left the room and returned five minutes later with a weird look.

"Your Emmanuel is coming here by 11am tomorrow," he said gently. My heart instantly jumped, but I quickly composed myself wondering what he was up to.

11:30am the next day, I sat between Samuel and Emmanuel in my room with a heavily coloured face.

I really didn't believe Samuel could have the mind or morale to invite Emmanuel in such manner and I equally never dreamt I would ever find myself in such unpleasant position.

If I had the power, I would have disappeared that moment, but I lacked such powers and so had no choice than to sit it out.

So loudly my heart pounded. So nervously I shook inside and so weakly I awaited my fate. But to my astonishment, Emmanuel just sat comfortably with a quiet smile on his face as he stared at us.

He looked very relaxed, calm and calculative.

"I had to lie and abandon my work just to get here due to the respect I have for you, Mary, and not because of the insulting tone and manner, your so called boyfriend used in inviting me. Please I didn't come here for a child's play, so you guys better be serious," he said, breaking the silence between us.

My dear Samuel instantly stood up, and stared at him with contempt and hatred.

"Thank you for honoring my invitation. I invited you only for one simple reason which is to tell you in Mary's presence to back off and leave her alone. She's now my girl and I will forever fight for her interest and defend her. We may not have this opportunity again," he explained and warned seriously with fire in his eyes.

Emmanuel simply scoffed, sighed and stood up.

"Is that all?" he asked, "you really have tried, thanks for trying to be a man," he added with a sneer, bent by my side and pecked me before I even realized his intention. I instantly stared at him with shock and disbelief.

Samuel however was more than shocked. There was fire in his eyes as his fury rose.

The insulting calculative reply he got from Emmanuel coupled with the provocative peck he saw him give me, totally outraged and disorganized him, instantly turning him into a beast.

Without thinking he reached out, grabbed Emmanuel by the collar, and jerked him violently.

His action tore Emmanuel's shirt, who instead of retaliating, smiled and shook his head.

"What's the need being so violent? In case you are not aware, better know this moment that I have much more claim over Mary than you ever will. I guess she's yet to gist you about our dirty secrets. So my boy fighting over a woman will only send you to your grave pretty quick instead of helping you prove a point. Don't ever dare touch me again; I'm not your mate. Mary is my wife whether you like it or not. It's just a matter of time," he bragged, while Samuel stared at him furiously.

"You are just a shoe cleaner my boy, so better learn," he added derogatorily, before trying to leave. But Samuel couldn't bear the insult any longer. He pushed him so violently that he landed on my bed and almost hit his head on the wall close by.

I clearly saw what Emmanuel was successfully doing, he was purposely provoking Samuel, but I couldn't figure out what he planned to achieve with it.

Samuel however, expecting a retaliatory move from him, quickly grabbed a small kitchen knife lying on my reading table, making me fetch my strength and jump out of my bed.

"Samuel, have you gone crazy? Drop that knife," I instantly barked, throwing myself at him, but unluckily he misunderstood my action and stared at me murderously.

"Christ, so Mary you are now defending him. I have been the fool all along," he ranted with a raised hand which still held the kitchen knife.

I swallowed hard as I stared at him, totally disappointed. I never knew a gentle boy like him could ever turn into such an obnoxious fellow.

I sighed, left my room and rushed to the general balcony, intending to clear my head there. Surprisingly, Samuel followed me, breathing heavily as if he ran after a moving car.

Emmanuel also left that moment, even though I didn't see him leave. My head was fully heated up like a dynamite waiting to explode. I was totally upset with Samuel.

"Mary," he called out and grabbed me from behind. I instantly turned and faced him with anger.

"It's over," I muttered coldly.

"What!" he gasped with disbelief.

"I'm dead serious. Our relationship is officially over," I repeated.

"Oh Mary," he tried to protest, but I instantly freed myself from his grasp, rolled my eyes and moved to the other end of the balcony.

"Please don't Mary me again, the decision has been made," I murmured coldly.

"No no no, I can't take this. I can't survive this. I'm sorry for going over the line, please forgive me," he apologized profusely, holding me again.

"I know we both are going to suffer over this but it's best for us. Focus your mind on your upcoming degree examination. Perhaps things will get better for us before you are done with it," I said coldly.

"Is it a crime to defend and fight over what is rightfully mine?" he asked anxiously

"Yeah, it's a crime to fight over destiny. Whatever is written for us can never be changed, even if you fight a thousand times," I replied and ran back to my room.

I had no peace for the rest of that week because my dear Samuel wouldn't let me be. He was extremely hurt by my decision. He kept begging and disturbing me as if my decision would kill him, but I neither yielded to his pleas nor listened to Mariam who pleaded on his behalf. It was as if my heart was on lockdown. I felt nothing and had no regret over anything.

I must confess his mistake seemed to be the perfect opportunity that came at the right time, and I knew I was simply overreacting.

However, his Mum surprised me with a phone call on Thursday, inviting me over to their family house during the weekend. I found it hard to decline, because the good old lady had been very kind to me. But as I prepared my mind and myself on Friday, rehearsing how to behave at her house, I got another strange phone call from Emmanuel's mother seeking to have a little 'face to face' chat with me, else she would come calling at my lodge.

I also accepted her invitation and got the directions to her house, because I preferred visiting her instead of her showing up at my lodge. I however couldn't help wondering how she got my phone number.

In such a short period, I became a hot dazzling 'must-get' princess.

At 2pm on Saturday, I was at Samuel's family house.

"Do you still love my son?" Samuel's Mum asked seriously, scanning my face with her eyes. I breathed deeply and nodded.

"Yes, I still do, Mum," I murmured. But my reply had no effect on her and didn't stop her curious eyes from running through me.

I arrived at Samuel's house quite on time to assist the Mum in preparing lunch. Something I did out of obligation and the respect I had for the family.

However, Samuel had travelled home the previous day, expecting me to travel with him like we used to whenever I was visiting his family, but I declined his request leaving him totally surprised and scared. He feared I would embarrass him by not honoring his Mum's invitation, thus the happiness and relief on his face when I eventually showed up.

His Mum however was a bit cold and reserved as she welcomed me. I knew as a woman she was very disappointed by my behavior, but perhaps was forced to invite me because of her son whom she had to set aside her personal feelings to please.

"Are you really sure about that?" she asked. I breathed deeply, smiling nervously.

I was glad she sent her son away before questioning me, something only wise mothers with good experience would do. I equally felt she wasn't listening or paying serious attention to my replies, but was intently examining my facial expression with each reply I gave, as though she were a mind reader.

"If you are still in love with him as you claim, why break up with him?" she queried. I shrugged, calmed my excitement before pouring out my own version of the story.

"Your story is similar to what he told me. You both made mistakes so I see no sense in your decision. My son is seriously hurting and I can't stand it any longer. But I have ordered him never to beg you again because relationships are not built on pity but with good understanding. So tell me, how long are you willing to put him on hold and what's your plan for the other boy?" she asked inquisitively.

"Mum, whatever will be, will be. I promise to work out things with your son but I need a little more time to sort myself out. I still love him." I responded to her, deliberately avoiding a mention of Emmanuel. She shrugged and smiled weakly.

I instantly knew she wasn't convinced with my reply. I needed no one also, to tell me I had failed her test. She really read through me so easily. A strangely gifted woman she was.

She asked no other prying questions as I spent the rest of the afternoon with them before rushing back to my lodge amidst Samuel's pleas. I knew the way I left without spending a single night with them like I used to, further added weight to her suspicions.

"Polluting Samuel's mind would be her next line of action," I reasoned.

I was unable to sleep that night as I pondered over the whole affair. By 12pm the next day, I was already on my way to Emmanuel's family house with weird feelings in my heart.

"Whatever is written can never be changed", how foolishly I reasoned.

***

Emmanuel, his Mum and I sat at the dining table, eating the Sunday rice before us. I was very nervous as I ate my own share of the meal, and couldn't help praying for the lunch to end quickly.

"I'm really delighted you honored my invitation. You can't imagine how pleased I am," Emmanuel's Mum said to me sweetly, while I blushed and said nothing.

"We really do have a lot to talk after the meal, so relax and enjoy our hospitality," she added delightfully. I nodded with a calm smile.

My heart pounded furiously as I stepped into Emmanuel's family house that Sunday, guilt and fear totally consuming me without warning. I would have turned and ran back that moment, if not for Emmanuel's Mum who came out of the house, saw me and came forward happily. The joy in her eyes as she came running totally buried my guilt and fear.

"Daughter in-law," she greeted as she hugged me.

Emmanuel barely touched his food that afternoon as he kept staring and pleading with his eyes, but I pretended not to notice, even though I very much understood his plight.

A heavy rain however started immediately after lunch. Lightning and thunder striking like madness.

"Don't worry dear, the rain will stop before 4pm," his Mum assured me with a smile as she led me to a sofa. Emmanuel also excused himself to attend to some area of the building which was leaking under the heavy rain, leaving his Mum all alone with me.

"I know all about your story with my son. Trust me if I were in your shoes, I would have poured hot water twice on him before allowing him to explain himself. I don't blame all you are doing to him, but I swear by my honor, my son is really suffering over this issue," she softly said, held my hand and stared into my eyes.

"No matter how hard we try to fight or pretend, the truth is that the memory of our first love affair will always remain buried in our heart. Our first love is the bedrock upon which all other subsequent relationships are built. And just like a house will never stand without a foundation, our life will be meaningless without the story of how it all started. Our first relationship really shapes and dictates the direction of our future relationships. Without it, I doubt if we would ever have the wisdom or experience to control our hearts. I do know your heart is beating furiously as I speak to you now. I also know there is doubt, confusion and uncertainty in it. This is where an elder like me comes in. I will never wish you bad or deceive you, because any agreements we arrive at will equally affect my son either positively or negatively," she lectured. I shook nervously as I listened.

"What do you feel whenever you look at him?" she asked searchingly. I swallowed hard and shook my head.

"I don't just know, Ma. I can't describe what I do feel, because it's a mixture of hatred, compassion, fear, anger and happiness," I confessed. She breathed deeply with a smile.

"You still love him my daughter. Please don't fight it any longer," she pleaded with wet eyes.

I knew she was very right, but I instantly remembered Samuel; a boy who showed me care and love when I needed it.

"I really can't go back to your son because I'm already with another person," I sobbed. The good old lady closed her eyes, breathed deeply and drew me to her chest.

"I do understand dear. My sister experienced the same thing when we were teenagers," she murmured with a broken voice. I instantly raised my face and stared at her.

"Yes, my dear, I speak from experience. The best you can do for yourself is to follow your heart. Allow it to be the Judge. Marriage is not something built on pity or sympathy, but something built on solid love. Please, dear, let my words not look as if I'm rushing you. There is still enough time for you to think over everything. I have your phone number, so reaching you won't be a problem. Just know that if you should accept my son, we will quickly arrange the marriage ceremony," she concluded with a smile, leaving me totally lost and confused.

The heavy rain finally stopped around 6:15PM messing up the road and making it very untidy to thread on. I was stranded.

"Our road wasn't this bad last raining season. It's as a result of the red soil poured on it by the contractors handling the construction," Emmanuel explained as we stood outside minutes later.

I had insisted on leaving after the rain stopped, declining his mother's pleas for me to sleep over, but looking at the road I knew I wasn't going anywhere that Sunday evening.

Chapter Thirteen

The clouds were thick and heavy. Somehow the rains had not finished the business. I retired back since the road was too bad to use.

Emmanuel's Mum gave me an old lovely pink night wear which I didn't know where she got it from. I thanked her, took my night bath and relaxed in the guest room.

I was swiftly carried away by my thoughts as soon as I lay down that I neither noticed when Emmanuel came into the room nor when he sat on the bed.

"Hey Mary," he greeted. I instantly sat up and stared at him suspiciously. His smile calm, but intense.

"I will be heading to town as early as 5AM tomorrow because of my work. I hope you can wake up by that time so I could drop you at your lodge before going for my own business. It all depends on our road anyway. Let's just pray the road gets a bit dried before dawn," he said calmly, but before I could reply, a heavy thunder went through instantly jolting us. Rain started dropping on the roof once again.

"Oops" he exclaimed, while I smiled, even though I had no reason to.

Before I knew what was happening, his lips were on mine. I heedlessly surrendered completely to him and he took advantage of me once again.

Minutes later, we silently lay bare beside each other, totally exhausted and weak.

Finally the sense of deep peace that overtook me during our lovemaking quickly began ebbing away. The implications of what had happened hit home and slapped me intensely.

A tide of guilt and self loathing swept through me.

"I have betrayed Samuel," I sobbed.

What bittered me the most was that Samuel never even went this far with me all through the while were together. He'd always wished we kept the love making aspect till our wedding night. There I was giving it freely to someone who didn't even deserve me. I was so ashamed of myself.

Is this how my relationship is going to end with Samuel?

"Don't cry my love; I know you do believe in destiny. This was destined to happen and nothing would have stopped it from happening," Emmanuel whispered to me, but I was inconsolable because I knew what I did was beyond pardon.

"How do I face Samuel after this? How do I stand in his presence? What will be his reaction when he finds out," I wondered sorrowfully.

"Baby, stop crying. The deed has already been done. It's now left for us to mend the rest," he pleaded.

"And how do you suggest we do that?" I asked with tears.

"I'm very serious about marrying you; all I need is just your consent. Leave the rest for me and it will be history in no time," he begged passionately.

"I can handle myself. I perfectly knew what I was doing when we made love," I said to myself like a lost soul.

"Oh Mary, stop talking nonsense," he consoled and kissed my hair, "We are in this together, count on me for anything," he spoke calmly, making me stare into his eyes. I saw sincerity, fear and uncertainty in them.

"All I want is for you to be the mother of my children. I say this with all sincerity. Open your soul to me baby. I need not only your body, but your soul and spirit as well. Please make me yours," he begged.

"Emmanuel please let me be, I'm still very troubled and confused," I sobbed.

"Why is it so difficult for you to accept me my dear, why?" he asked eagerly.

"It's difficult because I owe Samuel a lot. He was by my side when you abandoned me. He filled my spirit when I was weak, and defended me when you weren't there," I poured out. He instantly blushed in shame.

"I may not be very much in love with him like I used to, but I'll still be loyal to him until he sets me free," I added, while he stared at me with a coloured face.

"What nonsense are you saying?" he asked curiously with trembling lips.

"I'll be very honest with him; I'll confess everything that happened tonight once I go back to my lodge tomorrow. If he breaks up with me over it, so be it, you can then have your chance," I promised, leaving him in a terrible shock.

"Are you out of your mind? Surely he will end things with you but I don't think he will let you go without first breaking your head. The fury of a cheated guy is very enormous my dear. Are you trying to kill yourself? Mary what has come over you?" he asked anxiously. I smiled painfully and shook my head.

"That's the only atonement I can offer. If he kills me over it then you know we weren't destined to be together. Whatever will be must be. My life is already messed up, I have no reason to fear anymore," I cried remorsefully. He quietly stood up with a very terrible sick look and shrugged.

"Alright let's see how it plays out, but my dear I think you are not okay. Your grief has affected you badly," he murmured sadly.

"Whatever is written can never be changed. If something happens to me, then know it was destined to happen," I replied with a weak smile. He nervously dressed up and left without another word. So much shaken he was as he left the room that night.

"My God, I hope I'm not insane?" I prayed as I waited for Monday.

***

Emmanuel dropped me in front of my lodge. I thanked him, opened the front passenger's door and tried to alight, but he quickly grabbed my left hand and stared at me.

"Please Mary, I beg you, don't do anything silly," he pleaded. I smiled and shook my head.

"As for my confession, I will go ahead with it. Don't you worry about me, Emmanuel, I can perfectly take care of myself," I assured him before alighting.

Walking into my room, I rehearsed all I planned to tell Samuel. It really wasn't easy making up my mind for such deed, but like I told Emmanuel, nothing was going to stop me from going ahead with it.

Just like fate would have it, I ran into Samuel at the staircase, he was going downstairs to fetch water but instantly froze when he saw me. There was suspicion and relief in his eyes as they fell on me, while I nervously returned his look and greeted him.

"Mary, where are you coming from? I know you aren't coming from your house?" he asked inquisitively.

"Of course, I'm not coming from home," I replied quietly, left him and climbed the stairs. He quickly followed me, abandoning the water he was on his way to get.

"So where did you go?" he asked when we got to my room.

"Do you really want to know?" I asked calmly as I sat on my bed. He stood beside me, scanning me intently with his eyes.

"Do I still owe you any explanation concerning my movements? Isn't our relationship officially over?" I asked with a dirty smile. He scoffed and bit his lips.

"I see you are trying very much to harden your heart, no problem, but I still insist to know," he muttered.

"Alright since you insist, I spent my Sunday at Emmanuel's family house and I'm just coming from there," I opened up coldly. His face instantly coloured. There was shock, pain, disbelief and sadness in his eyes as he stared at me.

"No it's not true," he murmured with a broken voice, sat on my bed and covered his face with his palms. He never cried out but I knew he wept in his heart.

I stared at him clueless on what next to say or how to behave towards him. He sat with his face covered for about fifteen minutes before composing himself and drawing close to me once again.

"Did he, did he touch, touch you?" he stammered nervously. I was instantly torn between telling him the truth and lying to him. My confusion left me silent thus confirming his fear.

"Chai Mary, why, why nau?" he asked murderously with unshed tears misting his eyes. I was unable to stand his voice or gaze any longer. I quietly stood up and backed him.

"I don't deserve you Samuel. I really do care about you, but I neither understand my flesh nor the cravings in my heart anymore. Please free yourself from this torment and permit me to get another girl for you," I prayed with a fast pounding heart. But all he did was just shed the tears he unsuccessfully struggled to hold. I was very touched and would have cried beside him if not for the singular fact that I wanted him to let me out of his life.

Patiently, I waited for him to come around. I knew only one thing could happen that moment. Either he ends it like a man or ends up humiliating me. No matter which he chooses I knew nothing would make him want to continue with me.

Only a woman has the ability to send a great man to his grave without lifting a finger.

"But what really took you to his house?" Samuel asked minutes later, after cleaning his eyes.

"His Mum invited me for a little chat, but when I got there a heavy rain started and I was compelled to spend the night with them," I answered calmly. He swallowed hard with pain, his eyes soaked once again with tears.

I was uncomfortable watching him cry. I never knew guys could cry for love in such undignifying manner. Yes, I was very touched, but his tears only drew out pity from me, nothing more, and nothing less.

I knew he was very hurt and disappointed, but all I eagerly awaited was for him to cut the last rope loosely binding us.

"What do I do now?" he murmured unhappily,

"It's very obvious I do not deserve you, please purge me from your heart and permit me to find a suitable girl for you," I begged calmly. He breathed deeply and covered his face again.

"Seriously Mary, I don't know why all these are happening. We have a great relationship going between us, and now you are breaking my heart and making me the laughing stock of everyone. I hate to love you," he accused bitterly, while I closed my eyes as his furious bitter true words registered in my heart.

"I gave you everything you wanted and you are now paying me back with this unjust behavior. It's very unfair," he cried and stood up.

I anxiously stared at him with my hopes up. I was very sure he was about leaving my life for good. My eyes melted as I watched him walk to the door. Truly he never deserved such treatment.

He silently stood beside my door with his left hand on the door knob for some minutes, before turning to face me once again. He stared intensely at me for a while before advancing towards me with an unhappy look.

"I can't walk out from your life because of this single mistake, Mary. We have been together for a long while and you didn't give me cause to complain until Emmanuel showed up. I still do love you. Let's just forget everything and start afresh. I know you are acting the way you do because you are very confused. However I do appreciate your honesty. Not every girl will confess such a horrible deed. I do prefer the devil I know to the saint I don't know. I still do love you. Let's start all over again and put all that has happened these past few weeks behind us," he calmly said with a broken voice and eyes filled with tears, as he squatted by my side. I was deeply stunned, shocked, surprised and moved.

I never expected such response from him. It truly left me a bit relieved, disappointed and same time happy. In fact my confusion reached its peak that moment.

Chapter Fourteen

I was totally lost with no idea of where who to find me would come from.

If I had been told this was what would happen I would have doubted.

"No," I cried,

"Yes Mary," he beseeched, holding my face with both hands as he stared into my eyes.

"You owe me this chance and a whole lot, so let's give it another trial at least till I finish my degree examination and if things don't still improve between us, you can then leave for good," he added seriously, while I swallowed hard with a deeply coloured face.

There was fear, uncertainty and disbelief in my eyes as I silently stared back at him. I lost my voice that moment because his decision totally disoriented me. In all honesty, I owed him that benefit.

"What do I do now?" I wondered helplessly.

"Samuel won't let me go and there stood Emmanuel behind, breathing down my neck with fire and passion. I truly felt very committed to Samuel but my body yearned for Emmanuel, leaving my spirit utterly confused and my soul lost.

I really wasn't a girl who could afford dating two guys at the same time, something I do detest with passion, but I now found myself heading towards that dangerous path

***

I was lying on my bed, reading a Christian book on spiritual growth to calm my nerves when my phone rang. I dropped my book and glanced at my phone, it was Emmanuel calling.

"Hi, I'm in front of your lodge, can you come out? The gateman won't let me in," he asked calmly.

"Okay, I'm coming," I replied and hung up.

I gently walked to his car, opened the front passenger's door, entered and sat beside him.

"How far?" he asked, hopefully.

"Fine sha," I replied calmly,

"So how did it go?" he curiously asked, while I breathed deeply.

"I confessed to him like I promised, but instead of breaking up or getting angry, he simply forgave me and begged for us to continue with the relationship," I explained.

"Holy Moses!" Emmanuel exclaimed, snapping his fingers in disbelief.

"I seriously don't know what to do and you already know the condition I gave you last night," I added calmly.

He strongly held my left hand forcing me to stare into his eyes.

"I'm way too big to be fighting for your love with an undergraduate, but I can't deny what we had last night being very real. For that reason I will fight to the end just to have you and nothing will stop me either," he confessed seriously, making me gasp.

The evening breeze blew on us as we stared at each other silently.

"How do I redeem myself? How do I untangle myself from this rope? Should I hang myself with it?" I wondered deeply.

I can't believe he forgave you," he murmured inaudibly, breaking the silence.

"Yeah, because he loves me a lot," I replied proudly, "I know you wouldn't if you were in his shoes," I accused. He simply smiled and said nothing.

"I have to get going; it's already getting very late. I shouldn't be out of my room by this hour," I said and made to leave, but he still held me strongly, preventing me from leaving.

"So what happens to us?" he asked curiously,

"Emmanuel, I beg you, there is no us. I thought you promised to wait forever for me nau? Just keep waiting even if it means waiting till next life," I said a bit coldly. My reply made him loosen his grip. I instantly snatched my hand.

"Don't let your confusion ruin your life," he advised coldly and looked away. I eyed him silently before trying once again to leave his car.

"Mary, wait," he commanded calmly. I obeyed and stopped.

"I can't believe you went back to him after what happened last night between us. So you will continue the relationship with him like nothing happened between us, abi?" he asked,

"Please, don't insult me," I coldly replied and tried to alight from his car, but he quickly drew forward and grabbed my left hand once again.

"What if at the end it doesn't work out between you guys? Can you live with the memory that you had the opportunity to set things right and you didn't?" he asked, while I kept quiet, thinking over his words.

"I know you do love me, I know I still have the treasure I took away from you the very first time we had fun. Your Sam knows that as much as he knows you don't love him as much as you love me. He also knows he's fighting a lost battle, and I think it's only logical to think he is harboring something which you are too blind to see. What will you do if he finally abandons you at a point where there is no turning back?" he asked. I silently shook nervously.

"Please Emmanuel stop talking rubbish, you are hurting my feelings," I murmured with quivering lips.

"I tell you the truth my dear, for now you may seem like the perfect choice to him because he hasn't yet explored other possibilities. He is yet to explore the world my dear. Do you think he will ever forget the confession you made to him today? I tell you, he will never forget or push it away from his mind. He simply begged you because he had no choice. He did what he needed to do to protect his dignity. You can doubt me, but I swear you will remember this moment in few years coming. I'm a guy and I just told you how we guys reason. Guys groom love, we don't fall for love, but we can fall for lust. We fight most times just to protect our pride and not because we are in love," he poured out while I coloured and shook immensely. His words were hurting me, but I couldn't find the strength to run away, my ears eagerly listened.

"I have explored the world and returned because I discovered how unique you are. Can you swear he will return when he graduates and stays away from you for some time with the memory of your exploits buried in his head?" He asked.

"I can't lie to you, my dear. I know I love you, but do forget the silly remark I made about waiting forever for you. I can only hopefully wait two more weeks for you to think over everything I said and decide if to continue with him or start all over with me. That's all I can say for now my dear, so please don't hurt our future. He concluded and prayed.

I breathed deeply, summoned up my strength, and ran out of his car without even saying good night to him.

"I now have only two weeks to make the final decision and choose between the guy I love and the guy I owe my happiness, which way?" I wondered tearfully as I ran to my room.

I was at Mariam room later. Somehow I knew nothing she would say was going to make sense to me but I needed someone to share in my burden.

"I don't know what to tell you. Besides, my pieces of advice don't count after all. Do they?" Mariam asked after listening to all I told her concerning Samuel and Emmanuel. She truly was right that her advice wouldn't count, but I needed it notwithstanding.

"I won't involve myself in your affairs any longer, just follow your heart," she concluded.

Emmanuel was the person my heart yearned for and following it could bring my troublesome spirit to rest, but how to make Samuel understand was another heavy task which I truly didn't know how to handle.

It was very obvious he truly loved me, because he sacrificed a lot for my happiness and even forgave me after I cheated on him. But my greatest fear was that his love could fade with time, perhaps when nature begins showing itself on me. The age difference between us wasn't that much and I knew with time my physical appearance would change much more than his. Yeah, I knew it was a lame excuse but will he still love me when that happens? Can I risk waiting at least four more years for him to stand firm and be financially stable to cater for a family? What if he doesn't get employed within that period? What if he later changes his mind about me, will I be able to make up for the lost time? Will I be able to fall in love again? Will I ever forgive myself? No, I can't take such risk," I concluded thoughtfully.

Campus love affair is nothing but a fantasy life we create and plunge our youthful life in just for fun, pride and experimentation. It mostly has no longevity.

However, due to the great respect and commitment I felt for Samuel, I made up my mind to be with him till the end of his degree examinations, because I knew I won't be able to forgive myself if he lost concentration because of me.

But Samuel, thinking all was settling for good between us began spoiling me with gifts once again. At first I declined accepting them, but he kept insisting until I finally caved in. We cooked together and played like we used to.

The two weeks, which Emmanuel had given me to deliberate over his proposal, had elapsed and he was around to get my response.

I sat beside Emmanuel in his car, breathing quickly as I prepared myself to tell him my decision. Truly whatever agreement we were to reach that fateful evening was going to decide my fate and destiny.

God alone knows our destiny

"So how far?" he anxiously asked.

"I haven't been able to decide anything," I murmured with a fast pounding heart.

"Come on, don't tell me that. Have you forgotten I gave you only two weeks to decide? Why are you behaving like this?" he curiously asked.

"Emmanuel, I'll give you an answer at the end of this semester. Please allow me to focus on my studies. I can't be thinking of your proposal when I have examinations to prepare for," I entreated.

"I really don't know the kind of game you are playing, seriously I don't," he complained.

"So what's so hard about waiting an extra month for me to decide?" I asked.

"Because I don't understand you and I fear I may end up killing my time for nothing," he replied.

"If you truly love me like you claim then that shouldn't be too big a risk for you to take," I spoke defiantly. He breathed deeply, grabbed my left hand and stared into my eyes.

"Tell me the truth, what's happening please?" he pleaded. My lips quivered, while my bright eyes grew dim under his manly grasp.

"But for one thing, I would have said yes this instant, and gone with you to the very end of the world," I confessed.

"But what is it, Mary?" he asked, "What is it, my darling?"

"I cannot leave him, Emmanuel. I cannot leave Samuel by this hour; he's preparing for his degree examinations. Please be considerate. Yes, I'm with him, but it's more of a friendship thing, but you don't have to believe me," I explained. "It is the only atonement I can offer him. I owe Samuel this reparation for the evil I have done him and I must make it till he completes his degree examinations after which I will give you the answer you so much desire," I added.

He drew nearer and kissed my trembling lips, "alright I understand," he murmured coldly.

"Speak to me Emmanuel, it's hard, I know but tell me that I'm doing the right thing," I begged. He looked down and shook his head.

"You are cruelly doing the right thing" he murmured and switched on his car engine.

"I have to get going. I can't stand this anymore," he quietly added. I stared at him inquisitively but couldn't say any word.

I quietly alighted from his car while he furiously drove away without even bothering to give me a goodbye smile.

It was a very painful parting and I couldn't help but wonder if he would ever return for me.

I cried in my room as I thought over Emmanuel's behavior.

"Have I lost him forever? Did I miscalculate by pushing my luck to the extreme?" I wondered with tears.

I however devoted my time to being by Samuel's side as his degree examination slowly drew near, and as well pushing my fears and sorrows to the back of my mind.

In no time I got used to my new way of living; hiding my fears with smiles, and taking life as I saw it. Samuel also never gave me any cause to worry. He neither brought up any topic that would hurt my feelings nor ever mentioned Emmanuel's name. He truly was the ideal guy for any woman but he wasn't destined for me. I felt nothing but commitment, compassion and respect for him.

Finally, like the speed of light, the examinations came and were gone. Samuel was finally a graduate. I can't forget the night he graduated. How happy and over joyous he was thinking he could then focus on building his future together with me from thereon since he was then a graduate. Unfortunately my mind had long been made up. I had just decided to hang around him till he was done with his examinations before officially leaving the relationship and marrying Emmanuel.

"Seriously, Samuel, I do appreciate your love, care and everything, but this night is going to be our last together. I have tried to develop more feelings for you but have been unable to. Moreover, I know your Mum no longer likes me, so please tonight is our last." I plainly poured out to a visibly surprised Samuel. He gasped, left the bed and slept on the rug without saying another word to me.

The next morning I left his room before he woke up.

Even though what I did touched me, I was very glad I did it because I really couldn't guarantee my happiness with him.

He however, never did speak to me again.

He packed out of the hostel days later without bothering to inform me. I was a bit distressed because I really never wanted things to end that way between us and would have wanted for us to remain good friends.

Chapter Fifteen

Finally, I anxiously began waiting for Emmanuel who neither showed up nor called on phone. I soon wrote my second semester exams and travelled home for Christmas months later.

Three months I waited for Emmanuel, but not even a single phone call did I get from him. I lost hope, but for my pride I would have called him myself. Perhaps he wasn't in my destiny either.

***

I was cooking at the backyard when Mum ran into the kitchen very excited and full of smiles.

"Guess who just visited us?" she said happily.

"I can't guess Mum, please tell me," I begged.

"Emmanuel came with his parents. They are in the sitting room with your father," she said to me. I quickly dropped the kitchen spoon I was holding, without minding where it fell or the rough clothes I was wearing and ran into the sitting room where Dad sat with Emmanuel and his parents.

I greeted and welcomed them happily, my heart pounding furiously. Emmanuel stared at me with a smile, understanding the girlish shyness and sweet fear that had changed me into a timid girl. He stood up without wasting time.

"Mary, please I have something to tell you," he calmly said to me. My face instantly flushed at his words, eyes drooping with shy, sweet happiness.

"Let's go outside dear," he begged. I breathed deeply, looked at my Dad who nodded in approval, shrugged and left the room with him.

"I have borne my impatience and pride for the last three months," he said when we got to a lonely part of our compound; "but I now must speak to you, for I can bear it no longer, Mary. Oh, do not turn away from me! I can't hold my pride anymore. I love you and I want you to be my wife, darling; and I will love you, cherish you and spend my whole life in working for you. I have no hope so great, so sweet, so dear, as the hope of winning you," he poured out.

I made no answer. Yet my silence was more eloquent than words.

"It seems a strange thing to say, but, Mary all the time I was away, my heart was really with you," he confessed. I listened with a happy smile playing round my lips, my eyes drooping, while my face flushed and turned from his.

"You are my fate, my destiny! If only you will say yes to me, your love would incite me to win name and fame, not for myself but for you. Your love would crown a king. I beg of you, say yes to me this instant. Surely great love wins great love and there could be no greater love than mine," he begged desperately.

It was at this stage that our eyes met. The next moment he clasped me to his heart, pouring out a torrent of passionate words– such words, so tender, so loving, so full of passion and hope, that my face grew pale as I trembled and listened.

"It's love that makes life. Just say yes to me and by Easter we will get married," he proposed.

I raised my eyes to the fair, calm heavens, and infinite happiness filled my soul, a deep, silent prayer ascended unspoken from my heart.

"Yes, Emmanuel, I accept you," I finally opened up with tears.

He smiled happily as we hugged each other, but deep down I still felt an uncertain fear.

With a whimper of relief he smiled at me. His face was absolutely ashen, his lips white, as he pulled me savagely into his arms, folding me into the safety of his body, cradling my head, then cupping my face in his hands and tilting it upwards.

His eyes moved feverishly over my face as if he wanted to reassure himself I was really there.

"Thank God," he murmured as he bent his head, pressing his lips to my hair.

"I thought I'd lost you again," he confessed.

"But what kept you away for so long?" I asked curiously.

"It was my pride my dear, it ate me up like a terminal disease, but I eventually overcame it and came running with my parents. How do I make up for my complete and utter crassness?" he asked remorsefully. I looked away.

"I got this for you," he said, as he let go of me for a moment, pulling out something from his pocket.

"Now I want to do it properly, before anything else happens to come between us," he smiled as he held out his hand. In the centre of his palm lay a golden ring.

"Mary," he pulled me gently back into his arms.

"I love you," he murmured.

"I will forever love you, cherish you, comfort you and protect you," He kissed my middle finger.

"I will honor you and make endless fantastic love with you for all the days of my life." Holding up my third finger, he slid the ring onto it.

"If you will have me," He prayed. Through a shimmering veil of tears, I gave a soft laugh.

I was so happy, and so thrilled, because all my dreams were coming to past. What else could I wish for?

Together we walked into the sitting room to break the joyful news to our dear old parents.

Emmanuel made the necessary first payment which showed that he had reached an agreement with my family, just like our custom demanded, before collecting the list of items required for our traditional marriage, promising to show up three weeks later for the first stage of Introduction.

Unfortunately, it never happened as we planned.

Chapter Sixteen

Precisely two weeks later, I got very terrible news which almost killed me.

It truly wasn't the kind of news I was expecting at that stage of my life, neither is it the kind of news you guys are eager to read.

Mum walked into the sitting room, with a heavily coloured and drawn face. My heart leapt as I noticed her state.

"Mum! Are you alright?" I asked curiously.

"Don't mind me, I just received a very terrible news from a relative," she replied and walked to her room. I nervously ran after her.

"Just allow me be, dear, your Dad will be in a better position to break the news to you," she begged when she saw me enter her room. Her words panicked and got me more curious, instead of soothing me like she expected.

"Mum you are now getting me more worried," I held her hands, staring into her eyes. My heart pounded furiously as I wondered what could make her look so sick and nervous.

"Mum, I insist you tell me, please," I begged and shook her hands.

"Alright fetch me a glass of water, I'm very thirsty," she ordered. I ran to the kitchen, filled a glass cup with water and ran back to her room.

She smiled reassuringly after drinking the water, breathed heavily and caressed my hair,

"I will tell you the news I just got, my dear. It really isn't terrible like I earlier said, but just a bit surprising. So promise me you will behave like a matured lady when I open up to you," she asked of me.

"I promise I will behave, Mum," I managed to mutter anxiously.

"Do you know Emmanuel has a child?" she broke the news to me like a question. I couldn't believe my ears.

"Which Emmanuel?" I asked fearfully,

"Your Emmanuel of course," she replied. "We had to ask around, in order to get first hand information about the family we are giving out our daughter to, and ended up getting this piece of information from a relative married in his Village," she explained, while I bit my lips as sadness, disbelief and pain instantly filled my heart.

Mum clearly understood my condition, drew my head to her chest and patted me like a baby.

"You shouldn't feel very bad. You can still go ahead with the marriage if you love him well enough to overlook the little hindrance. The child is a girl and I heard the parents never accepted both the little girl and her mother," she consoled me.

"Mum, please don't talk like that," I cried. "How did it even happen?" I heard myself asking.

"According to my source, he got the girl pregnant before going for his NYSC. That should make the child a year or more, I guess," she replied. I felt empty, sad and weak.

"No wonder he was very anxious to marry me quickly. And his Mum even hid it from me," I cried bitterly.

I felt played and betrayed, very uncertain of my future with him. It was at this point I knew I had lost my future and I regretted ever leaving Samuel the more.

The next evening, Emmanuel was in our house as if someone alerted him of what we discovered. He came straight to my room, sat on the bed and stared at me nervously. I sat up and stared back at him with a ferocious look, breathing heavily as I tried so hard to control my emotions. "Dear, please calm down. The love I have for you is very sincere. Listen to me darling, please listen to me," he pleaded nervously. "You are just so heartless. You thought you could hide such a big scandal from me, didn't you? Or have you cooked up another lie? Come on, spit it out," I said angrily. He shuddered as my words hit him hard, forcing him to look down remorsefully. "I couldn't get myself to tell you about it because I was very scared of your reaction. I couldn't risk losing you over a silly mistake," he uttered earnestly. "The girl was a mistake and I have nothing to do with the mother anymore, please believe me. It was only a one night stand I regret ever doing. Please don't judge me over it. Judge me for who I'm and not for whom I was, please," he begged. "I want to see the little girl and her mother. I want to see them before I say anything else to you," I requested seriously. His hands shook as he tried to hold my waist. He breathed deeply and stared at me curiously. "Don't tell me you are already changing your mind over us?" he asked with a coloured face. I scoffed and looked away. "I'm not happy with you and I have nothing else to say until I see your little daughter and her Mum," I concluded bitterly. "This is so unfair Mary, why do you insist on seeing them? I can't let you see them, I just can't," he murmured sadly, while I forced out a dry smile.

I demanded to see the girl and her mother because I wanted to get first hand information, concerning the level of relationship they enjoy with him. Moreover I really couldn't bear standing between anyone's happiness especially when a child is involved. I hate seeing a child grow up without a father. I know to some people it matters not, but to me it matters a lot.

"What you are asking of me is very outrageous, I can't do it. Moreover they are not living with me and I can't take you to their house," he explained seriously. "Then invite her to yours or somewhere conducive for us to meet," I insisted. "Meet over what? And what exactly do you expect me to tell her? That my fiancée wants to see her? You are very insensitive to another person's plight. You only think about yourself and it isn't good," he accused bitterly. "I understood and was reasonable with you when you were virtually living with Samuel. Why can't you respect my feelings? In fact I can't stand you this evening, I'm leaving," he poured out angrily, stood up and left the room, while I silently reflected over his words.

"Oh my God, he just accused me of being insensitive and selfish. Is he right?" I gasped and wondered. Mum ran into my room few minutes later, with concern written all over her face, "I hope you weren't hard on him?" she curiously asked, while I picked my nose. "The poor boy is in bad shape, looking very troubled and sad in the sitting room. What did you say to him?" she inquired seriously. "I only asked to see his daughter before deciding anything, but he suddenly grew very intense and annoying. Imagine the boldness," I complained to Mum, who calmly sat beside me, held my left hand and smiled at me.

"You should have been more understanding and diplomatic with your request. Go talk to him dear, I believe you guys can sort things out unless you are changing your mind about him already." I rolled my eyes and smiled at her. "Oh Mum. The truth is that I can't help but feel for the child and her mother. I can't imagine what he told the poor girl before doing the deed which got her pregnant," I explained. "You are right my dear," she said with a nod. "You are always very considerate of other people's feelings," she said softly and I smiled. "But Emmanuel just accused me of being selfish and insensitive," I murmured. "Oh please. Go and settle with him," she stood up and dragged me to the sitting room, where Emmanuel sat with a drawn face. I quietly sat beside him. Mum smiled and left us alone.

"I'm very sorry for being rude. I never intended to disrespect you or hurt your feelings, but as your future wife I should know everything about you and I believe I have every right to know your daughter and her mother. Please don't deny me that, I beg of you," I pleaded calmly with all my heart. He looked away thoughtfully, breathed deeply and stared into my eyes. "Alright your wish will be granted. You leave me with no choice than to make it happen, but I do have a very bad feeling about it," he said with a forced smile, while I heaved a sigh of relief. "I will invite her to my apartment in town on Saturday, but I will be here on Friday evening to pick you up," He added. "No dear, I'll prefer you come on Saturday morning so I can bring my school things along," I requested humbly. "Alright I will be here very early on Saturday," he accepted with a dry smile.

"It wasn't that hard after all, was it?" Mum asked with a smile as soon as he left. I rolled my eyes and ran to the kitchen without answering her, praying silently that things work out between Emmanuel and I. With the direction things were taking, I was a bit scared of my future with him. Nervously, I waited for Saturday which slowly approached like a snail. I woke up that day with a huge boil under my armpit. Creepy, isn't it?

Emmanuel showed up by 7:30am, beaming with smiles as he walked into our house. "Please don't be too hard on him or to yourself my dear. Behave like a good girl which you are, okay! I will be expecting you next weekend," Mum advised as she kissed me goodbye. I finally left our house that Saturday morning with Emmanuel, who had a new aura of self confidence in him. Silently he drove to the capital, while my thoughts kept me company as I thought about school, my future, my life and even about Samuel.

"Who knows how he is?" I wondered with mixed feelings.

He silently drove without bringing up any conversation, until we got to my hostel an hour and half later.

"This place surely brings back memories," he murmured with a smile as he killed the car engine. "Surely it does," I responded before alighting. He dutifully helped me carry up my luggage and organize my room. Fifteen minutes later, we headed to his apartment which was just few kilometers away from my lodge.

 It was the first time I was visiting his apartment, and even though he wasn't a stranger to me, I still felt a bit nervous, making him stare at me curiously, as soon as we arrived. "My dear why do you look so tensed?" he asked with a smile. "Because it's the first time I'm visiting a place you rented with your money," I replied with a smile. He scratched his head and laughed. "So my family house you visited months ago isn't mine abi?" he joked. I smiled silently. His three bedroom apartment really was very simple and a bit scanty, perhaps because he was yet to save enough money for adequate furnishing. The chairs in the sitting room were plastic however a plasma screen television, sound system and some simple gadgets adorned it. My heart skipped five beats when I got to his kitchen and saw lots of dirty dishes piled up in a big basin, waiting to be washed. I had no choice than to get to work immediately, even though he weakly objected.

"I'm the happiest man in the world right now. You are so lovely, so beautiful, so enchanting, and I will forever worship you," he kept singing, with hands in his trouser pockets, as I did the dishes. "When is she coming?" I asked after a while, interrupting his praises. He glanced at his watch and shrugged. "She should be here by now. She promised to come before 11am, now it's past twelve," he replied. "I hope you didn't trick me into coming to your house?" I asked suspiciously. "Of course not," he answered innocently. At exactly 2pm his phone rang, "She's at the door," he said to me after answering the phone call. He rushed to the entrance door and opened it. My eyes followed him expectantly, while my heart pounded very fast.

A young girl soon walked into the sitting room carrying a child with her. She froze as our eyes met, while my heart melted with pity. She looked so young and beautiful, but was wrapped up in sadness. "I'm so glad you came," Emmanuel said to her with a quick smile. She nodded and stared at me suspiciously. "Meet my fiancée, Mary," he introduced me to her. "Mary, meet Stella, the mother of my daughter," he said to me. I rose up politely, reached out and made to carry her baby, but she drew back and stared at me murderously. Tears quickly formed in her eyes, while her lips shook. "What? Jeez, I can't believe my ears. Your what?" she asked Emmanuel, who instantly looked away, placing his right hand on his head. "You are his fiancée eeh?" she asked, facing me angrily. "Yeah and I asked him to invite you so we could straighten things out," I murmured nervously, "Straighten what?? You must be mad if you think you can involve me in your little prank. He abandoned his responsibility for your sake and you are now here playing some saint. I'm not a fool, sis. I'm not," she sobbed. "Calm down dear, I have your interest at heart. Sit down let's talk please," I begged. "I can't calm down, and I can't stand this scene either. I'm leaving this moment, but I assure you that I will be back. Go ahead, be his fiancée, and enjoy yourself," she poured out with tears, before running out of the sitting room with her child.

Her action and tears touched my spirit, but I was at same a bit angry at her for not calming down and listening to me.

"You have now seen for yourself what I have been avoiding. I knew it wasn't a good idea getting you to meet her. You see?" Emmanuel murmured bitterly, while I looked up at him searchingly. "Now what do you think?" he asked, "I don't just know. But I'm having a very bad feeling right now," I replied calmly. He quickly drew close and held me. "I think it is better we get married before Easter. Let's move our wedding forward. I can start making the necessary arrangements instantly," he proposed nervously. I breathed deeply, raising my eyebrows. "I think it is better we shift it farther. Perhaps move it to December," I said thoughtfully, while he gasped with disbelief, "or maybe until we settle issues with her," I added cautiously. "What's there to settle with her eeh?" he asked sadly. "A lot, my dear, a lot, because I don't believe she will just sit calmly and watch us get married like it doesn't concern her." I replied with a quick smile. He quietly sat on the floor, looking dejected and sad like a man who just lost a big fortune. Even though I appeared calm and relaxed, I was far from being pleased with the direction

I feared our relationship was heading. I felt like visiting a fortune teller that moment.

 I finally pushed aside my fears and prepared soup and stew for him. Emmanuel however stayed with me in the kitchen, cracking silly jokes as I cooked. At exactly 6pm, after I was done cooking and resting, I rose up to leave, "I have to start going," I said to a surprised Emmanuel, who quickly drew close and held me. "Why the rush? I thought you were spending the night here? Tomorrow is still Sunday," said pleadingly, "I know but I just don't want to spend the night here," I replied with a frown. But before he could insist, someone knocked on his door. "Who could it be?" he asked. I scoffed and rolled my eyes, "Who are you asking?" I asked him. He smiled, walked to the door and opened it. I felt a funny sensation as soon as he got to his door which made me walk up to him. I got beside him and stared at the door way, there stood Stella standing with her baby in her arms. I froze with surprise and shock, while the girl stared at me coldly, "I didn't know you are still around," she said to me coldly. I breathed deeply, forcing out a smile. "Oh yeah, I'm still here," I replied, grabbed Emmanuel by the waist and rested my weight on him. She shifted her gaze to Emmanuel who was yet to mutter any word. "Too bad because I have nowhere to spend the night and my little daughter is hungry," she added seriously. Emmanuel instantly looked at me while I shrugged. I knew the unfortunate girl was out to make trouble, but I wasn't in the mood to oblige her. Moreover every decision was on Emmanuel to make. "Won't you guys let me in?" she asked curiously. I rolled my eyes, bit my lips and returned to my chair. She shoved Emmanuel aside, and entered the sitting room, using her baby as a shield. I stared at the young girl speechlessly, clueless on how to follow her up, while Emmanuel walked up to her with a drawn face.

"I don't know your plans, but you are not spending the night in this apartment," he said to her. But she simply scoffed and smiled. "May God, have mercy on you. You are now deceiving this young girl the way you deceived me. Anyway come and carry me out if you can, I'm ready for you," she dared him bravely. But unfortunately her eyes betrayed her with tears. "Stop being obnoxious and uncivil, it isn't going to get you anywhere," I advised her with a frown. "Stay out of this, it's none of your business," she fired back furiously. "It's my business dear, because I compelled him to invite you," I responded. She scoffed, dropped her child on the floor and advanced towards me. "You want to make it your business right? So shall it be," she threatened murderously, while I shook with fright. It was very obvious she was extremely angry and dangerous. Judging by how furious she was, I knew I was no match for her.

Emmanuel instantly came forward, grabbed her from behind and dragged her towards the door. She shoved and resisted but Emmanuel's grip was stronger. With a last minute ferocious move, she leveled her two legs against the wall as soon as Emmanuel got her to the door, using the wall as leverage to send him backwards. Emmanuel staggered backwards loosening his grip a little, which gave the angry girl an opportunity to bite his hands without mercy.

He screamed with surprise as he felt her bite, flinging her away from his body, before descending on her with two slaps, which brought out a loud scream from the fighting girl. But instead of backing out, she launched yet another attack, diving forward with intention of jerking him through the mid section; a very silly move which earned her a knockout punch from an angry Emmanuel. She fell backwards, grabbing her jaw as tears freely flowed down her eyes. Her little baby began crying that moment, moving my fragile heart and getting me more confused, as I contemplated on going for the child or not.

Emmanuel advanced towards her again to render more finishing blows, but I sprang up and held him. "I will have none of this Emmanuel. What has gotten into you?" I asked nervously, "I'm merely defending myself from this witch. Didn't you see she could have easily taken me out?" he answered angrily. "You laid your hands on me, Emmanuel? You guys don't know me, I will be back shortly," the angry girl threatened and left the house leaving her baby behind. A cold shiver instantly ran down my spine. "What's she up to?" I wondered fearfully. I knew Emmanuel also asked himself the same question. What was her plan?

"What do we do dear, what do we do?" I nervously asked as I picked up the crying child. "I don't know my dear; I guess we have to wait for her to come for the child. I hope you aren't planning on leaving me here alone?" asked Emmanuel, fearfully. "Of course not, how do you think I will leave this child with you," I answered. He heaved a sigh of relief.

Anxiously, we waited for Stella to show up. The clock soon struck 7:00pm, but she was yet to return. 8:00pm I got very worried and anxious, "What if she isn't coming for her baby?" I asked Emmanuel who simply shrugged with confusion. "There is no way she could have left for the village by that hour, I have a feeling she's at her brother's apartment. Her elder brother is a police ASP, a graduate in police uniform," he explained lightly. I simply stared at him, extremely shaken and confused. "I think I still remember the house address the brother once gave me when I was settling her case with the family. I will return the child first thing tomorrow," he added with a blank expression. "Seriously, Emmanuel, how did you get yourself involved with such obnoxious girl?" I asked curiously. He silently scratched his head and shrugged. "It's a long story my dear. A very terrible mistake which is slowly eating me up like cancer," he muttered weakly, collapsed on a chair and sighed. My stomach growled and bit, I was very hungry but had no appetite whatsoever to eat. I knew Emmanuel also felt the same way.

 Exactly 8:38pm, we heard gentle knocks on the entrance door. Emmanuel breathed deeply, stood up and opened his door. I instantly gasped as I saw him leap backwards, while two uniformed policemen jumped into the room, grabbing his trouser by the waist. Another guy on mufti gently walked in with Stella by his side.

"There she is," I heard Stella say, pointing at me, "she's the lady that orchestrated the whole plan to steal my child," she said to the policemen. My heart instantly skipped five beats. I felt like disappearing that moment. "What's happening? How dare you guys barge into my house to intimidate me? I know my rights," Emmanuel yelled. "Then you have to start calling your lawyers, because you are in for a very big case; Assault and battery, attempted murder and child theft. My friend you aren't getting easily away this time. You can't humiliate my younger sister and get away with it whatever be her fault." The guy on mufti barked angrily, while the two policemen dragged us into a waiting police Van.

***

My first visit to Emmanuel's apartment was a big disaster as it earned me a night at the police station. Emmanuel was thrown into the cell as soon as we arrived at the police station, while I was left to cool off at the counter behind the reception desk. "I just don't want to punish you further because like my sister, you are just another unfortunate victim in this whole mess. I would have thrown you into one of the cells as well," Stella's brother said to me. I nodded gratefully and thanked him. "Yes sir, thank you sir," I murmured nervously. My thoughts kept me company all through the night as I wondered what Emmanuel's fate would be. By the look of things, I saw that Stella and her brother were very ready for a tough battle.

Mosquitoes however never allowed me to think properly, I kept slapping myself as I battled them all through that restless night. I was in a very terrible state the following morning. God being so kind, the morning arrived earlier than I had imagined it would.

Fortunately for us, Stella's brother arrived at the station very early, and sent for us. I hastily walked into his office, while Emmanuel was dragged in minutes later. He looked tired, scared and nervous, but fortunately his body wasn't in anyway tampered with. "You know before I joined the police force, I used to be a very bad player? I did everything unthinkable just to get down with a girl, but I neither for once laid my hands on any girl nor got any pregnant. You know why? Because I used my head," he lectured Emmanuel with a smile. "I'm so sorry mister, but you went too far with my sister this time around, and I'm going to deal with you to the extent you end up losing your job. You know banks hate getting involved in scandals, huh?" He asked Emmanuel, who instantly frowned and looked away. "I already have mapped out my plans, first I will call the press and some popular bloggers I know, give them the story I prepared about you with the caption, "BANKER COOLING OFF IN POLICE CELL AFTER

TRYING TO KILL GIRLFRIEND", OR "BANKER TRIES TO KILL AN INNOCENT EIGHTEEN YEAR OLD GIRL IN HIS APARTMENT" or better still, "BANKER TRIES TO KILL BABY MAMA FOR ANOTHER" he tilted his head sideways and poured out evilly, while I gasped. "What do you think will become of your job after such news is made public, or what do you think the state prosecutor will do after learning of such case?" He asked with a mischievous smile. The look on Emmanuel's face was terrible. It was very obvious he was extremely scared. He looked like someone who just saw a ghost. "I have evidence, plus pictures of my sister's battered face and doctor's report," he continued.

"Please what is it you want?" Emmanuel nervously asked, interrupting him. The young police officer simply licked his lips and smiled. "Hmmm, what do I want?" Stella's brother repeated and scoffed. "You used my sister, got her pregnant, made her unmarriageable, abandoned and broke her heart and I kept quiet and never for a day confronted you. When my parents managed to fetch you for talks, you showed up, claimed responsibility and disappeared like a ghost, I still never bothered you. I took care of my sister without complaining, but I guess because of our soft nature and the way we handled everything, you thought you could do as you like, thereby further insulting my family by inviting the innocent girl to your house, so as to beat her up and snatch her baby," he narrated calmly, while Emmanuel nervously watched him like a rat watching a friendly cat. "What do you expect me to ask for, eeh?" he asked Emmanuel, who simply shrugged silently. "I can't force you to marry my sister and I can't as well allow you walk away from your responsibility over her and the little girl," he added seriously. "But this isn't a case settled in the police station. Can't we do it elsewhere, like in your house or village?" Emmanuel asked pleadingly, "Oh yes, but I don't trust you, moreover my sister is the person pressing charges and I fear you might spend more time here with us," he replied with an evil smile. "Oh goodness me! I beg of you, don't do this to me, I can't afford to skip work even for a day, please," Emmanuel begged nervously, while I nodded in support. "Alright, but there is still one more thing you have to do, if I'm to allow you guys to leave," the young officer added and licked his lips. "You have to sign some papers, it's just like an undertaking which you have to accept before I let you have your freedom," he added as he brought out two envelopes, which he placed before Emmanuel. "All you have to do is just to sign both of them, you go with one copy, and I keep the second copy for myself," he explained as Emmanuel went through the papers. "You don't expect me to sign this crap do you?" I soon heard Emmanuel ask with a raised tone. "How do you expect me to suspend my upcoming wedding, till I settle issues with your sister?" he asked angrily. "Oh, so the wedding rumors are true? Yes sir, my request is very reasonable, because that's what any sane man will do. For the sake of my family's pride and for the sake of tradition, you have every reason to sit down and settle with us, before rushing into another marriage. Moreover, which church will wed you when you are yet to resolve your problems eeh? My friend you better sign the two papers, because it's that or nothing," the young officer sprang up and barked loudly, hitting the table with his fist. My heart skipped a hundred times over. It just looked as if someone was blowing an air of misfortune towards my happiness.

How will this whole issue end?

Chapter Seventeen

"I hope my girl is free to leave?" Emmanuel asked quietly with his eyes on me. The young officer calmed himself, sat on his chair and breathed deeply as he stared at me.

"She's free to leave, I have nothing against her for the moment, but I will be forced to involve her if we are unable to reach an agreement," he replied. Emmanuel instantly smiled at me.

"I hope you heard him baby? You are free to go outside and wait for me," he said while I blushed and shook my head.

"Don't worry about me. I think it is better I sit here and listen to everything," I replied with a calm smile. He shook his head and stared into my eyes.

"I insist dear, please go outside and wait for me, please I beg of you," he pleaded seriously. I breathed deeply, stood up and left the officer's office without another word.

I wasn't happy that he asked me to leave, because I was keenly following the whole drama like a soap opera. Perhaps he did it to protect me, or did it to hide something from me.

As I angrily left the police building, I ran into Stella at the entrance. She smiled as soon as she saw me and stopped.

"Hi friend, good morning," she greeted. I felt like ignoring her, but my anger overcame me. I stopped and stared at her furiously.

"What's good about the morning?" I asked angrily.

"Oh a lot dear, today is Sunday don't you know? Oh how would you remember since you spent your night in a good hotel huh," she replied with a smile.

"Whatever you are planning, just know that bad things don't last. You will be judged for your actions. Better know that," I preached and made to leave, but she strongly held my right hand, which surprised and stopped me.

"Where is your child? You want to fight me again huh?" I asked with burning eyes. She scoffed and shrugged.

"Come on babe, cool off, we should be friends instead of enemies," she said with a changed tone.

"I don't have your time, so please get behind me," I yelled and turned to leave.

"Whether you like it or not, you will be seeing more of my presence and I advise you leave that obnoxious Emmanuel and make something good out of your life now that you still have the time, because I will make his life miserable and burn who ever stands on my way. I think I have given you fair warning my lady. Emmanuel ruined my life and I will go to any length to ruin his," she threatened seriously. I froze for a while, meditated over her words and walked away silently.

A new fear erupted in my heart. I had no doubt she was serious with her threats.

"Can I stand her? What else is she planning? Is there something I'm yet to find out about Emmanuel?" I wondered fearfully, my legs shook while my heart pounded furiously.

151

I calmly left the police station and waited for Emmanuel in a shop close by. I anxiously waited for forty five minutes, but he failed to show up.

Nervously, I returned to the station with my heart pounding furiously and fear engulfing me immensely. But luckily I met him at the entrance door, the spot I earlier had a little confrontation with Stella. I heaved a sigh of relief as I stared into his eyes.

Stella's brother was standing by his side. They stared at me for a while without saying anything.

"You are free to go, but do know that my eyes are on you," he finally said to Emmanuel as they shook hands.

"No problem," Emmanuel murmured, held my hand and made to walk away with me.

"Can I have a word with you, please," I heard Stella's brother ask with his eyes on me. I stared at him nervously, breathed deeply and shrugged.

"Okay," I muttered and walked towards him, while Emmanuel watched suspiciously.

"You have seen nothing of what we call life. Your boyfriend is false in heart, in mind, in soul; he has a false flattering tongue, false lips, and false principles. You better be careful," he advised seriously, surprising me with his bluntness.

"You better watch your tongue mister," Emmanuel instantly barked, reached out and dragged me away.

"Don't mind the idiot," he nervously said to me as we left the police station.

We said nothing to each other until we arrived at his apartment minutes later.

"So how did you finally settle with them? Did you sign the papers?" I asked curiously. He breathed deeply, and shook his head.

"Please I rather not talk about it, Please," I heard him say.

"But I have every right to know, don't I?" I asked.

"Please allow me be, I'm very hungry," he murmured with an angry tone.

Without another word, I dutifully prepared and served breakfast, which he ate hungrily. My thoughts kept wandering to and fro as I watched him eat. I wasn't as hungry as he was, because my heavy mind veiled my appetite.

"I'm still eager to know how you settled with him," I anxiously said, hiding my anxiety with a gentle smile.

"I'm telling you no story, so please bother me no more. I have enough problems already," he replied coldly. I stared at him angrily, stood up and bit my lips.

"I think you are hiding something nasty from me. It is better you open up now or…"

"Or what?" He cut me short before I could complete my statement. "Mary, give me some space please, I'm choking," he added defiantly, getting me extremely annoyed with his remark.

"Fine, I'm leaving. You know where to find me," I shouted at him, grabbed my bag and ran out of his apartment.

I was extremely angry and down casted. I felt very bad because he treated me like an insignificant child. I understood his problems were telling on him, but to be treated in such undignifying manner was something I couldn't stand. He also never cared to run after me or call me back.

I was almost in tears when I got back to my lodge minutes later.

Fate however added salt to my wound, by making me run into Samuel as I ran up the stairs with tears in my eyes.

I froze in shock as I stared at him, got hold of myself, looked away and ran past him to my room, but he surprisingly came after me, catching up with me as I stopped to unlock my door.

"Happy Sunday, Mary," he greeted politely.

"Hello Samuel," I murmured nervously. He breathed deeply, drew close and studied me silently. Luckily, I managed to open my door that moment, and rushed into my room without another word. He however joined me in my room, throwing me into great tension with his undesirable behavior.

He was the last person I expected to see or talk to that moment and I was extremely ashamed that he saw me in a very terrible state. My heart pounded furiously as I fell, face on my bed, backing him rudely, and praying silently for him to leave. My prayers weren't answered. He simply stood patiently waiting for me to get hold of myself.

"Please let me be, I'm not myself, please," I finally heard myself say to him.

"You look very troubled, dejected, broken and lost. What is happening to you?" he asked curiously. I bit my lips and sighed deeply.

"Sam, please leave me alone, I'm very tired and weak," I murmured, sat up and faced him with a coloured face. His eyes melted as he looked into mine, he came forward and squatted by my side.

"Did he hurt you again? Tell me, what did he do to you? I see pain and unhappiness in your eyes?" he asked searchingly, making me blush and look away. I was extremely embarrassed and ashamed.

"Why should you care, please leave," I said to him, but he gently shook his head and held my hands.

"Old things have come to pass, my dear. This is a New Year and 'a New Year Brings a New beginning'. So don't worry about the past, you can still count on me for anything," he sweetly said, as I looked into his eyes and saw hope. The only thing missing that moment was a soap opera music.

My heart pounded furiously as I tried to say something, I opened my mouth but no word came out. I swallowed hard and looked away, deeply embarrassed and confused.

"Mary," Samuel called my name softly, breaking my heart and flogging my soul with his voice. He really behaved like a good Christian, very forgiving and caring, making my conscience flog and bite me without mercy.

The way he offered his help totally broke me into two. I couldn't believe he was ready to help after how I betrayed and dumped him just some months ago.

"I don't deserve your help, sympathy or anything, please just go, I beg of you," I finally managed to mutter, shaking and surprising him with my outburst.

"You are too proud and it isn't good for a girl," he said with a very sad face. I breathed deeply and touched his left cheek.

"You are a very nice guy who deserves the best things in life. Each time I look at you, my conscience hurts because I instantly remember all the bad things I have done to you, so accepting anything from you will kill me. Please just let me be, moreover I'm not in any terrible situation that needs help, believe me," I explained calmly. He bit his lips and stood up.

"I broke my pride and most importantly, I did what every guy will frown upon, by coming back to see you. But it is okay," he murmured regrettably.

"Oh no Samuel, don't say that," I cried, stood up and hugged him tightly. "You are a very nice guy and I know God will repay you somehow," I prayed,

"We don't choose who we fall in love with. It's something that happens without influence, and when it happens we leave everything just to follow our heart. Sometimes we end up with the wrong person but believe me, that's it," I poured out as I held him tightly.

"And what happens to a guy who falls in love with a girl who happens to love another?" he asked,

"Honestly I can't answer that," I murmured with a heavy heart.

"I wronged you. I scammed your family and broke their trust. I'll be at your family house next Saturday to apologize and seek forgiveness from your family," I heard myself say. He instantly broke away from me, stared into my eyes and rubbed his face with his palms.

"Will you actually do that?" he asked curiously,

"Of course I will. Moreover, it's the only way I can atone for my sins and be free from the evil touch of misfortune which has befallen me lately," I confessed.

Was there ever anything seen like love and sorrow meeting together in a place?

The pure love of Samuel's noble heart, and the keen sorrow in mine brought sadness, bitter than death upon us as we stared at each other.

"Alright then, I have to get going," Samuel finally said. I nodded with a faint smile.

"Thanks again for checking up on me. I hope you will be at home on Saturday?" I asked meekly,

"Of course I will," he replied, breathed deeply and turned to leave.

"Sam, please wait," I begged nervously, forcing him to stop, turn and stare at me curiously.

"I have cute course mates who will be willing to have a relationship with a guy like you. Should I arrange one for you?" I asked nervously. He breathed deeply and shook his head.

"Never mind, thanks," he objected.

"Are you sure?" I asked seriously.

"Yeah, I'm sure. And I'm also sure that someday you will regret leaving the only boy who truly loved you," he answered, turned and left without another word.

Well, he was right. I was regretting it already, he just didn't know.

I took a long shower, freshened up and had a little nap. However a loud knock on my door hours later, woke me up. I lazily answered my door and smiled brightly as my eyes fell on Mariam.

"Thank God you are back. I missed you dear," I happily cried as we hugged each other.

"Me too," responded happily.

Even though our friendship wasn't as strong as it used to be due to my strange affair with Emmanuel, we still maintained a little closeness and still shared a unique bond which kept us together like sisters. She never supported how I got back with Emmanuel, but it never stopped me from sharing my fears with her.

"Could you believe Emmanuel has a daughter," I announced as she walked into my room.

"Don't say that, jeez!" she exclaimed with surprise, settled down on my bed with both hands on her jaw and listened keenly. I gently sat beside her and narrated the latest story of my life to her.

"Damn this is so weird and unbelievable," she murmured and shook her head after listening to all I poured out.

"My dear I think you should run away from that guy, unless you are willing to risk your life over him. Moreover it isn't too late for you, since you haven't given him much commitment, or slept with him after that careless night you spent at his family house last year," she advised seriously.

"You are right, but I just can't do it and don't ask me why, please," I said seriously. She scoffed, shook her head and held my left shoulder.

"I think you are being insanely stupid, seriously," she scolded.

"You used to be a level headed, intelligent girl, but it seems you are getting stupid as you grow older. Please don't take it the wrong way, but I have to tell you the truth," she added with a serious look.

"What is love without happiness? And what is happiness without a bright future?" she asked, forcing me to look away in confusion.

"There is no doubt you are in love with Emmanuel, but where is your happiness, and how will your life turn out in few years coming?" "This is no soap opera; we are talking about your life. Youthful love fades with time, but happiness and bright future can make it last a life time," She advised with burning eyes.

"You are like my sister my dear, and I know you have a very good but weak heart. Do you think you stand a chance with Stella and her numerous antics? Answer me. Moreover how you are sure Emmanuel won't abandon you at the last moment?" she asked seriously, "After all, he is not bad at it," she added. I silently swallowed hard, completely lost in confusion.

I was lost, disoriented and disorganized. Instead of helping, Mariam choose to dismember me with her frightening questions. But sometimes a truthful reality is very painful and horrible to imagine.

But could she be right with all she's just said?

Chapter Eighteen

The morning was bright, beautiful and busy with students hurrying around for their lectures.

I left early for school and attended my first lecture as a final year student. It really brought brief happiness to my life, making me put all my fears behind me. I religiously faced my studies.

Tuesday evening approached very fast, bringing Emmanuel with it. I was writing an assignment when I heard someone knock on my door. I thought it was Mariam, but was a bit surprised to see Emmanuel standing nervously with a coloured face.

"Hello," I greeted coldly, before paving way for him to enter my room. He calmly sat on my bed, while I returned to my assignment which I faced seriously.

"Why haven't you been answering my calls?" he asked calmly,

"Because I have been very busy, which you can see for yourself" I replied coldly.

"I came to apologize for the way I treated you on Sunday," he said slowly.

"You have nothing to apologize for, I perfectly understand," I replied.

"Seriously I'm yet to get myself, it hasn't been easy for me," he tried to explain, but I interrupted him rudely.

"You have no need to explain yourself, let's forget about it," I muttered without caring to look up at him. He stood up and drew close to me.

"I know you are still angry with me, tell me isn't it so?" he asked searchingly.

"Please I'm not angry. Allow me to concentrate on my assignment, I still have four pages to cover," I replied with a slightly raised tone.

"I have to get going, it's almost 6pm. Do take care dearest," he said, stood hesitantly for a while before leaving my room. I never bothered to say goodbye to him.

***

Mariam dragged me to a boutique which was just few houses away from Emmanuel's apartment, giggling happily as she showed me the gown which made her drag me out by that hour.

"Mary isn't it beautiful? I couldn't afford waiting till tomorrow, because I can't risk losing it for anything," she explained happily as I stared at the beautiful gown. She was right; the pink cute thing was well designed with a lovely material.

"You are right dear, the gown is worth the trouble," I replied with a smile. She laughed and quickly paid for it.

As we left the boutique minutes later, I begged her to accompany me to Emmanuel's apartment which was just few steps away. She wasn't happy about it, but had no choice than to follow me.

But you can't imagine the surprise, shock and anger I felt when the door to Emmanuel's apartment was opened by no other person than Stella, three minutes later.

"Oh, dear, good evening. I guess you are looking for Emmanuel, he went out minutes ago," Stella giggled with bright eyes. I breathed deeply, as I desperately tried to control my temper.

"It's in our best interest to keep our thoughts quiet. Let's go," Mariam cleverly whispered, before dragging me away.

"Aren't you going to leave a message," I heard the obnoxious Stella ask as we left the building.

I wasn't myself as we headed back to our lodge that evening, because not only was I jealous and angry, I was also very doubtful about Emmanuel's intention towards me. My thoughts wandered aimlessly, while the police officer's advice came rushing into my head.

"You have seen nothing of what we call life; your boyfriend is false in heart, in mind, in soul; he has a false flattering tongue, false lips, and false principles. You better be careful," he had advised me on Sunday, but I choose to ignore him.

"Could he be right?" I wondered, "No no no Emmanuel won't be so stupid as to get back with her. There must be a different reason for her to be in his house," I fearfully concluded.

Mariam and I didn't say much to each other when we got back to the lodge. She soon retired to her room, while I settled to sleep, but I kept tossing on my bed uneasily due to my unhappy thoughts. Unable to control my emotions I dialed Emmanuel's phone number only to get the greatest shock of my life.

"Hello Mary," he answered in an unusual manner seconds later,

"I came to your house earlier in the evening with my friend, didn't Stella tell you?" I asked. He kept quiet for some seconds.

"No, she didn't tell me anything. Why didn't you wait for me to return or call my cell phone? I could have rushed home instantly," he asked,

"There isn't any need for that since your wife is already there," I answered coldly.

"I wanted to explain this to you the last time I came over to your place, but you never granted me the audience," Emmanuel Said.

"I am sorry to tell you this, Mary; things cannot work between us anymore. Let's go our separate ways. I am so sorry."

He was still about apologizing when I switched off the phone instantly. I couldn't believe my ears. I was totally confused on the next thing to do. I cried hell out that night and was lost in thought all through the night that I never knew it was dawn already. I was to visit Samuel that day with Mariam accompanying me.

Together with Mariam, I headed to Samuel's family house, very scared, confused and nervous, but I was consoled with the fact that I was doing the right thing.

"I think coming here is a bad idea, we should go back," I nervously muttered when we got to the gate. Mariam scoffed and shook her head.

"No! no! no! madam, we aren't going back. We are already here and we have to go ahead with what brought us to this place.   Moreover it was hundred percent your idea," she said to me as she firmly held my left hand.

Without another word, we walked into the compound, cautiously with prayers on our lips. We soon got to the entrance door, stopped and stared at each other nervously.

"What are you waiting for? Come on, knock on the door nau," she urged as though it were a very simple thing to do. I took a deep breath, shrugged and knocked gently.

Two minutes later the entrance door was flung open by Samuel's mother, who stared at us with a serious but not mean look. She breathed deeply and admitted us into the house politely, even though her smile was heavily cloaked with sharp coldness.

I searched for Samuel with my eyes as we walked into the sitting room, but unfortunately couldn't locate him, thus making me more uncomfortable. His Mum's pointed gaze unsettled me greatly. I nervously settled on a couch with Mariam dutifully beside me.

"My son told me you wanted to speak with me," the old woman announced after some minutes had gone by. I breathed deeply, rubbed my knees nervously, nodded and smiled.

"Please, where is Samuel?" I asked calmly,

"I sent him on an errand. I thought it was I you wanted to speak to," she said with a burning gaze.

"Yes Ma, his presence is not really needed. I was simply checking on him," I murmured with a coloured face.

"Actually, I came to tender an apology," I stammered, while she drew forward on her chair, feigning surprise and pretending as if she wasn't aware of what I came to do. Her action truly unsettled me further. I was so nervous. I was doing something I hadn't seen any girl do and the old woman was making it more difficult for me with her intense behavior.

I tried to continue with my apology but was unable to. All I was able to do was just throw a nervous glance at Mariam who gave me an encouraging smile.

I never knew tendering a sincere apology could be so difficult.

Just at that very moment, Samuel walked in with a lady right beside him.

"Hi Mary," he greeted.

"I'm glad you came as you promised," he said as he sat on a separate couch with the lady beside her.

At this point I was getting jealous seeing Samuel with a lady beside him. I garnered some confidence and apologized immediately to her Mum.

"It's no problem, Mary. I forgave you long time ago."

"I hope you will be coming to my son's wedding next week," she asked?

I was shocked and surprised at the same time!

At that moment, Samuel threw a card at me; it confirmed what her Mum just said. It was an invitation letter to his wedding with the lady right beside her. Unfortunately, it was too late for me. I fainted immediately after reading the content of the invitation letter.

I woke up after sometime with Samuel and Miriam by my side. Tears flowed freely from my eyes as I had a flashback to what Samuel told me when we last met, "And I'm also sure that someday you will regret leaving the only boy who truly loved you.”

-THE END-

————————

Morale

Loving with the heart alone mostly will end in tears. Love with your heart and with your head.